BEGAT WHO BEGAT WHO BEGAT

Dear Kim-
So wonderful to meet you at last. Thanks so much for having me. I wish you the greatest success with your new book. Looking forward to it!

~~Marcus Pactor~~

Astrophil Press

at University of South Dakota

2021

Layout and design by duncan b. barlow

Editing by McCormick Templeman

Astrophil Press at University of South Dakota
1st pressing 2021

Library of Congress Cataloging-in-Publication Data
Marcus Pactor
p. cm.
ISBN 9780998019963 (pbk. : paper)
1.Fiction, American
Library of Congress Control Number: 2021939996

http://www.astrophilpress.com

STORIES:

For Julie, Sam, and Miriam. You have given me everything.

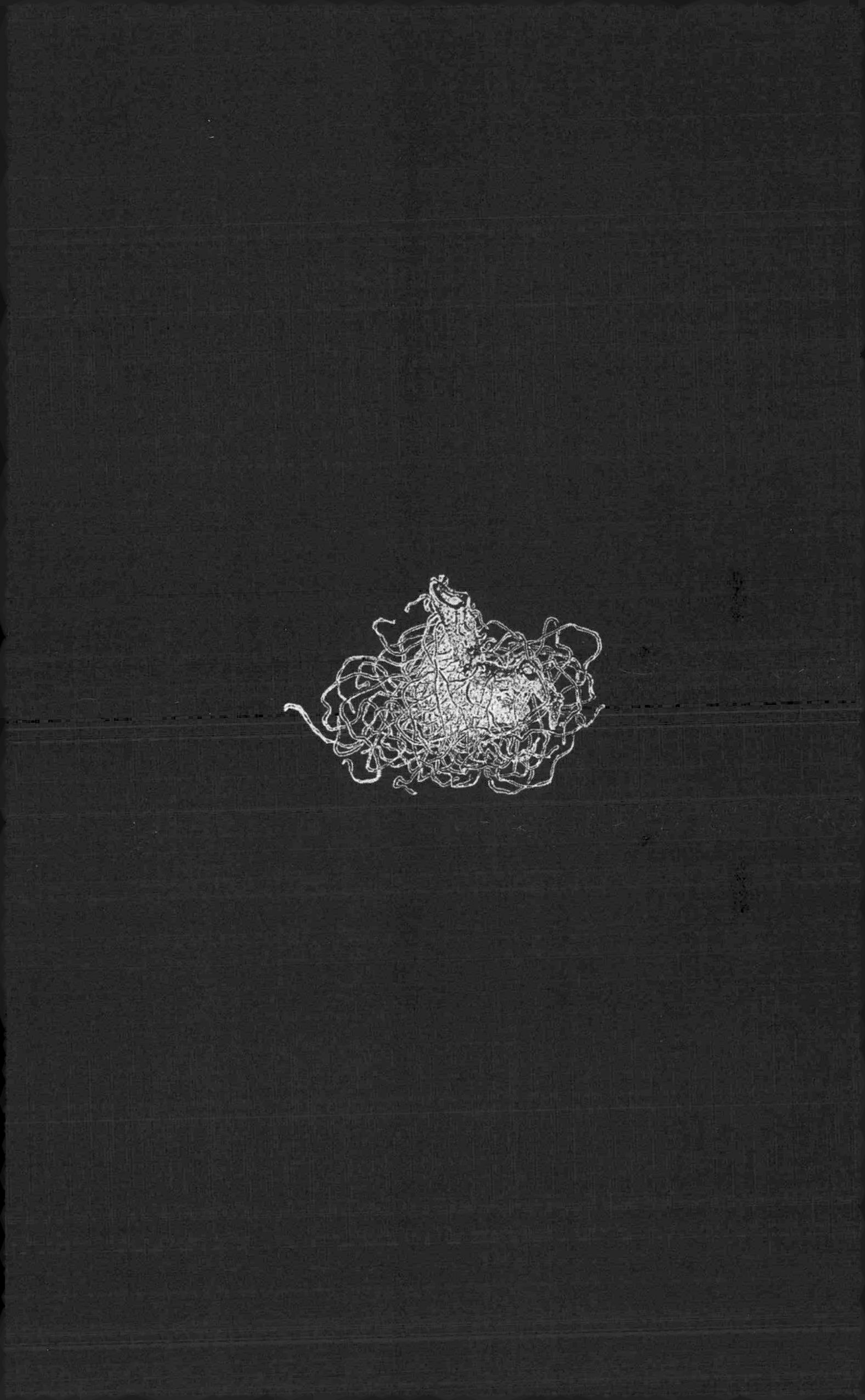

A Giving Toilet

GABRIEL DESCENDED THE STAIRS and presented me a bowl full of his teeth. He lisped the number of dollars he expected from the Tooth Fairy. I helped him rinse his mouth, then returned him to bed, medicated Lila, and soothed the woken daughter. The next morning, Gabriel counted his money but could not gloat. Staff doctors at the hospital turned us over to the distinguished resident from Bombay. He read Gabriel's x-rays and declared our son's voice box gone. "Poof," he said, clapping and turning his palms up to the light. We were not amused. The resident explained that such things happened sometimes in the woods of Chota Nagpur, less often here.

He sent us home after a week of fruitless tests and samplings. He asked to be kept informed. An article could be published; a documentary could be made.

In the downstairs bathroom that evening, old scratches in the toilet's base turned into cracks, those cracks turned into deltas, and water ran through my socks.

I never told Lila that, before I installed the new toilet, a golden spider crawled from the floor register. She would have looked at me foul if she knew I had not bagged it alive for money but instead ground it into the tile. I swept the goop and fragments into the brown hole which led, I figured, to a landfill or ocean or limbo. Then I set the wax and leveled the toilet and bolted it down over the portal. I hacksawed the bolts' rough ends and caulked the toilet's base and attached the water cable and opened the valve. The liquid treble feedback sound of the refilling bowl reminded me of TV news anchors interrupting my dreams. Gabriel fetched me to eat before I could test the flush.

Lila baptized the toilet after lunch. The children were banging pots and I was rinsing dishes when a moan grew loud beneath the house, followed by a pop in the bathroom. Lila squealed.

Soon our gathered family surveyed a toy duck, preserved in shrink wrap, floating on its side in the bowl. I washed the find in the sink and sliced it free with a box cutter. I massaged and sniffed it. No excretory residue adhered either to it or to my fingers. Then Lila tested it with close-up eyes and hard sniffs and hot-potato hands before agreeing that it posed no harm. The daughter once again ignored my best goo-goo faces and sounds. She giggled, though, when Gabriel squeezed and flew the duck at her nose.

In the living room, the children continued their play while Lila cuddled me on the couch. She had the tenderness of a noodle, though I never said so aloud. She would think I considered her bland. She would ask me if I thought I was the marital sauce. No, the word "noodle" simply came to mind whenever she touched my knee. Later, I touched the crown of the toilet. Later still, I touched the forehead of my sleeping son, and I hoped.

[Night]
During night feedings, I often sang mindless songs or whispered tall tales to the daughter. We rocked in a chair given to us by Lila's dead uncle. The deceased had given us a great deal, though he had failed to leave us money in his will. The story was complicated and despised.

In this near privacy, I thought of the nurse whose hand had grazed mine at the hospital's commissary, reaching across me for a blueberry muffin. I had never been touched by a nurse so white and fat. In the cradle of my arm, the daughter slept and sucked. She could not express much. She had not hit many of the benchmarks listed in Lila's books and articles. I sang of a princess who turned into a fish, then a tiger, then a hawk orbiting a mountain. Afterward, I described the mountain's wondrous shape. I detailed its icy peak.

In spite of regular lever-pulling, the portal did not open again for days. My hope waned until another moan and pop attended Gabriel's flush. He came out beckoning like a happy dog. He led us to a shrink-wrapped, blue-diamond necklace moving in the bowl. I cut it free and trusted it to my son, who offered it to his mother. Lila sniffed it and let her young gentleman clasp it round her neck. He smiled rosy gums and broken roots. The diamonds shined like crumbles of sky.

That afternoon, she wore the necklace to our city's most neglected park. There grass grew from rocks and rocks grew from grass. Trees slumped more than stood on a line to the east. The basketball goal had neither backboard nor hoop. Puddles had the haze and glow of motor oil. Ducks flapped noise on the womb-shaped pond. At the water's edge, frogs gathered round a bike tire. Its upper half cooked in daylight; its lower half waved like a ribbon on the water. Somehow the sun made wonder of that wretched earth. I pushed my family on the big spinner colored with graffiti. They rode with open, laughing mouths, though Gabriel, of course, could not laugh.

A pack of older children advanced from the court. I worried over the necklace, but they were after Gabriel. They made him a crown of grass, built an altar of brush, and brought him a frog and a sharpened stick, but he waved off their plan, and they were amazed by his mercy. He tossed the stick forty yards end over end. It landed spike down on an anthill. A glory floated about and through him.

I watched from the tree line, where I had followed the women. The daughter crawled over the roots of a dead oak. Lila tugged my shirt and said that I must flush the toilet after lunch tomorrow.

[Night]

In the dead uncle's chair, rocking easily for any and all to see, I felt songless. The daughter's mouth hardly moved on the bottle, though she groaned whenever I pulled it back. The longer she took, the more I soured. I could never sleep after her leisurely drink sessions.

The uncle had bought the rocker as well as the baby's crib and dresser. He had bought most of Gabriel's furniture, the living room couch, and the lamps scattered across the house. He would not let me slip him twenty bucks here or a hundred bucks there. Sometimes, though, he let me wire a fan or replace a rotten board on his property. On breaks from those jobs, I looked in vain for signs of company: a second razor in the shower, a tampon in the trash can. He could not tell a screw from a screwdriver. He had more liver spots than real teeth at his passing.

I relayed these dumb facts to the child.

Then I thought of the nurse. Her blond hair. Her berry perfume. Her smothering white fat smothering me.

Say a man stops at a hospital's commissary for lunch. The moment he tongs a lukewarm chicken thigh, he spies a nurse paying for her tray of slop. Later, he brings her a muffin. And so on. Should have skipped to the so on.

A song came to me. I declined to share it with the girl.

[Night]
Gabriel slept fine. I watched his back inflate and deflate. The toy duck stood guard atop the bed's mantle. It had nailhead eyes. The tooth money was crumpled in a bowl beside it, the same bowl Gabriel had used to deliver his teeth to me. Beside the bowl lay the crown of grass. The bowl had been a mainstay of silent games of blackjack between him and the uncle. They tapped a card to hit and waved a hand to stay. They played for pennies and, whenever Gabriel won, he dropped his spoils into the bowl. He stirred those pennies with his hand, making a sound like metal rain.

Gabriel must have learned his stoicism from their method of play. He had not saddened once over his lost teeth and, in fact, enjoyed pointing at what he wanted of the world. He did not want much, apparently, beyond his sister's duck. I touched the money. Then Lila entered, stroked my arm, and pushed her chest against mine.

[Night]
She rolled from me toward the window and faded from coitus to dream. I sat up, filmy in the crotch and bitter atop the covers. At the climax, the nurse had filled my mind.

Now I wondered what the golden spider's bite could do. Its venom might transmute guts into gold. Then noodle and children and mortician and nurse would tear at me with forks and knives. They would set my newly golden muscles and bones on the prospector's scale. I retain—even now—a low opinion of justice.

The uncle seemed to make money from air. Less alchemist than diviner, he had seen before almost anyone the importance of floppy discs and, later, their obsolescence. Yet he had seen little of the world. Its weather and landscapes and cultures did not stir him. He played cards. He called and took calls from his broker. He went barefoot through our house on summer days. The daughter, like him, had large gaps between her toes and dulling brown eyes. My wife said to forget the debts. He said money did not matter. But, on his last Valentine's Day, I pulled him into the garage to show off a pair of earrings. He asked me what I knew of thrift. I did not ask him what women he knew.

I excused myself from the table before biting into my roast beef sandwich. The family escorted me to the bathroom door, smiled as I closed it on them. They joined me inside after my flush. Soon a moan and pop brought a green thong from below. It could not have fit around Lila's hips. It could never become a voice box in Gabriel's throat. We watched incoming water carry it around the bowl until it floated like seaweed before us, and a monogrammed "B" on the crotch became legible. Blue sequins bordered the letter.

Gabriel fished it out and made a dripping pendulum of it. My daughter splashed the forming puddle. Lila conveyed several unpleasantries to me.

"What?" I said.

She went upstairs.

The children and I returned to the table. Before my flush, Gabriel had been slurping milk-soggy chocolate cereal. He would continue a soft food diet for another week, when his dentures would be ready. At other meals, he ate strawberry ice cream and, less often, his sister's jars of pureed fruit. He would not try the distinguished resident's under-the-table jelly, a mixture of vitamins, herbs, and elephant shavings favored by some villagers in Chota Nagpur. The doctor claimed its heartiest devotees survived well past their centennials, but Gabriel had not listened past the word "shavings." I could not blame him. The mixture smelled like a zoo cage left unattended for several summer days. I had raised my sandwich level with my mouth when Gabriel set the thong on the table. I told him to put it in the trash. He dipped it in his bowl, waistband first, as though he was releasing a fish into a pond. He swirled it in the milk till the crotch flattened and spread over the surface. I dumped the bowl's contents into the sink and switched on the garbage disposal. Its blades chopped at the thong. They failed to eat it.

I poured him a second bowl. Gabriel let it soften, then wolfed it down. The daughter painted her tray with milk and pureed peas. Cabinet doors vibrated. The refrigerator hum sounded male and soothing. My stomach seemed to fold over my bladder. I took the children to the living room and overturned a bin of toys. The children played till Lila returned. She wanted to take her kids for a ride.

I unscrewed the bathroom's floor register and gloved my hands and drew from the duct a morning's worth of Cheerios, gauzy sheets of webbing, and three golden eggs like misshapen marbles, all of which I flushed.

Then I stretched the thong across the pit of the sink. It smelled like chocolate milk and disposal bottom. The "B" looked ripped by a gator's claw. I considered working it further with a box cutter and tossing the shreds into a neighbor's backyard, then taking the family out for barbecue.

Instead, I reinstalled the floor register and returned to the table. At last, I would eat what I could of my sandwich. I set aside the hardened bread and wilted lettuce and faded tomato, and chewed the softer slices of meat, which were still flavorful with veggies and Creole mustard. The cabinets had not quit their vibrations, but they bothered me less now. The thong lay over my knee, letter down. I would have liked the uncle across from me, eating a sandwich of his own. I would have given him the thong to sniff.

I found, under the bottom slice of roast beef, a golden egg. I washed it and the remainder of the sandwich down the drain. I rinsed the other dishes, hid in the master bathroom, and found a second egg in my pocket. I sent it down the bathtub drain. I showered till I heard the ticking of legs in the drain grow loud.

I felt easier and more certain after I dressed. I waited in bed for the last egg to reveal itself and hatch, for the newborn spider to bite my calf. Later, I woke to pressurized quiet. My ears felt encased in plastic shells. I did not budge. An idea remained from my dream: to call the daughter by name. She had not yet had a chance to flush the toilet. My family would gather round. I would help her press the lever. The moan and pop would herald the necessary gift. I would wire the new box to my son's throat. Gabriel would beg in his old voice for ice cream. Lila would push her breasts against me, and she would be enough, and I would be enough for her. The daughter, too, would know the weight and value of my heart.

Good Fat

For weeks, our son had been spitting food. His boluses resembled gray lumps of paste. They hardened too quickly for me to get a mop and bucket into cleaning position. I had to sing him into a nap before I could scratch a putty knife at the mess and soak it with Pine-Sol. The clean floor was no relief. I foresaw him starving and our family becoming featured subjects on the evening news.

My wife discovered that he would eat anything smothered in guacamole: fried eggs, cut-up chicken, shreds of spinach, whatever the government recommended. Toward the end of our sixth consecutive pleasant meal—on Shabbat—my wife professed that guacamole was putting good fat in his brain. I had never heard of good fat, but I was willing to believe. He was eating, and we were eating meals hot from the oven again.

She said our brains were made of fat, mostly.

She had bought economy candles at the grocery. On the table, they burned down between us. Their tallow had too sweet a scent.

I said I'd better get at the screws.

Those screws had fixed a tension between us months before, because I was supposed to have had them sorted in Tupperware bowls before our son's birth. I kept thousands of them in the garage: drywall screws for indoor jobs, wood screws for outdoor jobs, concrete screws in case a neighbor with a brick house needed a hand. For my ongoing project, I'd acquired new and expensive screws online, from an exclusive site for tool aficionados. They generated enough cold to maintain their original shape and threading no matter what weather they faced. In general, my wife left decisions about screws and other garage business to me. Tonight, however, I felt my governance in jeopardy.

Maybe I should have explained to her the project: preservation of the dog. Despite six months in the chest among the screws, he remained identifiably a dachshund. I took his frozen paw and held it for some time. I worried not that I was a fool—I had long understood that—but that I was a fool because I had never eaten an avocado.

I asked him if I could have been an astronaut or TV personality had I consumed better food as a boy.

I asked if my lack of good fat explained my need to masturbate into a sock on Wednesday afternoons, a need which had been no more obviated by regular love-making than old-fashioned guilt.

I asked if good fat had been discovered with good science or if it was the product of fool brains fouled like mine by decades of bad fat consumption and, if so, did the cumulative effect of bad fat upon us imply that, somewhere in the world, there must be good fat to consume, whether in avocadoes or not, or were all our fool minds too set on binary possibilities to see what else might be profitable to chew down, like maybe red mulch, or were we too worried altogether about what to eat, given that we had already eaten ourselves into fools.

I asked if my questions had to make sense.

He did not answer.

His silence had been tolerable when all I had needed was his ear. But, that night, his tail felt too much like the hooked handle of an umbrella, his tongue like sandpaper worn to nothing. I extracted his eyes and found the remainder of face too dark.

It was spring, and in the dewy mornings I often brought my son outside to observe frogs lounging in the air conditioner's water discharge. Snails climbed the sides of the garbage cans and recycling bins. The latest and most enterprising snails had found a way into the garage. They might have been after the dog but, given their size and lack of limbs, I considered them a low-level security risk. My son's newfound mobility posed the real threat. One day, he would sneak out here alone and open the chest.

A paw-nail fell loose in my hand. It was a tender moment, like the time one of my dental crowns fell out during an act of love. Two years earlier, after my wife and I had finished our challah and wished the rabbi and our friends in the congregation a Shabbat Shalom, we went into the parking lot, feeling fine about the world. Streetlight cut through our car and, when we took our seats, our bodies. I put my hand on her thigh. We were well engaged when the crown slipped free. I do not believe my wife, caught up and ecstatic, understood what had come between our tongues. Perhaps she did, but chose to go on. We all want to go on, of course, once engaged. I deftly swallowed the crown without interrupting our fun. For a week afterward, I checked my stool to see when it passed. It never passed.

Our rabbi, on the other hand, died the next month, and we were not satisfied with the new hire, and our friends in the congregation became less our friends, and we did not like the other shuls in town. We tried our best to keep the customs on our own. We wanted to set an example for our son. On Friday evenings, we lit candles and said blessings, but we did not do well in regard to the law. I did not. Still do not. That Shabbat, I did not refrain from work with the screws, nor did I close the chest to pray, though I did pray: May his brain grow thousands of folds of good fat. May he use it and keep it long after mine turns to paste.

In the Weeds

Since P had gone missing, Berman had impressed his wife, the viewing public, and even the police with his stoicism. He administered a handkerchief to his person only in private, only when necessary. He continued to perform his professional responsibilities with his usual competence, and he continued to fulfill his duties as a husband and a property owner.

One morning, however, while he was cutting the grass, the lawnmower snarled and said, "Poor hoss...The TV ate your baby...It lured him with clown hair...pop eyes...danced, joked, promised...then its screen-mouth opened...you hear me, hoss?...it had one tooth...canine... bottom row...on the left...dirty white."

Berman slapped his right cheek and heard plain engine once again. He cut in neat rows, circling trees, keeping upright.

His lawn shared a backline fence with Tuttle's property. This neighbor fertilized his grass at the start of every season. He divvied up his yearly tomato harvests into gifts for families on their block, leaving green baskets full at their doorsteps. He had recently crossed—twice, unasked—into Berman's yard to pull weeds.

Berman tried but could not tamp down his envy for the man's aluminum shed. Its humming A/C was meant to cool a house. Clean, lanky Tuttle often carried a contractor's heavy duty trash bag into that shed and emerged later, slick and muddy and hunched under the bag's new weight. He would heave it into the cab of his SUV and haul it into the night. But when Tuttle came out at noon, he ambled straight to the SUV, waving good-bye to Berman as he passed. He wore a scarlet Polo shirt tucked into stonewashed jeans with the hems tucked into polished cowboy boots. His leather belt was buckled with a gold star that might have been ripped off a boy's sheriff suit. His new handlebar mustache appeared to have been glued on and made of moose.

Berman had once touched a dead moose. He and his stepfather were hiking to some Alaskan fishing hole, in heavy gear and galoshes, poles over their shoulders and tin cups of herring jangling in hand, his stepfather comparing the scent of their bait to that of a despised woman. Berman, in the tangy outdoors, believed himself likeable, courageous. Then they came upon the body—a hairy, humped shadow bleeding onto the path. Worms in its gut wound ate its bones and tissues. The moose's vacant grin reminded Berman of old men in suits. Its antlers had been amputated, leaving behind red, pus-filled bean shapes that both repulsed him and begged him to reach out. His stepfather shoved him forward. Berman set down his pole and tin. He stuck two fingers into the closest shallow hole, an icy, gummy little mouth. His stepfather should have said something life-directing or, at least, memorable, but Berman only heard white nature quiet.

Berman's lawn posed several unpleasant threats. Two gray mounds promised ant hell to the clumsy of foot. The recycling bin had not been overturned after a recent storm, and he could almost hear the mosquito eggs hatching therein. Among the thicker weeds, he could run over a stray baby bottle. Its plastic shrapnel would get lodged in his calves, though it would pierce no serious artery. Berman could mishandle the electric mower on a turn, severing the long cord, and he might forget to cut the power before snatching it. He could run over a deaf kitten, but never a moose, no matter its impairment.

It is perhaps too late to mention that he was already slobbery wet hot. It is perhaps too late to describe the paleness of the grass or the whiteness of the weedflowers rising alongside Berman's shed. Their roots and follicles made a tangled, wiry construction below ground. He could not picture its total shape, though he sometimes felt that he could map its near corner. He wasn't sure if he was fortunate or unfortunate that the feeling never struck when he had pen and paper nearby.

He had been in Tuttle's home twice. Each time, the faucets had been shined, the stove eyes wiped out, and a white lace tablecloth spread for company. Berman suspected that tablecloths were regularly washed and spread in the widower's home. A framed photo of

K stood in the table's center. Other pictures of her interrupted the paint of hallways and bathrooms. They weighed down mantles and end tables. In every picture, she posed alone.

On the first visit, Tuttle allowed P to grip his finger. The baby giggled at Tuttle's girlish pain sounds. L knelt beside them and smiled, though she could not entirely admire a man who served nachos without salsa.

On the second visit, Berman felt empty as air. He slouched in a love seat while the host poured tumblers of rye. L had stayed home, in bed, with pill dreams. Tuttle offered Berman a handkerchief and pressed one to his own foggy red eyes. They drank in earnest.

"A man," the mower said, "takes a bad turn with an electric mower—are you with me?—and severs its power cord. And that cord ends up in his neighbor's yard. This man don't unplug that cord. All that's an absolutely plausible result of grief. And that afternoon, his neighbor comes across that cord on his way from his back door to his SUV and, not knowing it's still live, takes it in hand. You tell me, hoss: What's the first hungry animal to approach the meat?

"Or suppose a bright baby develops faster than his parents could've guessed, so he turns out brighter and more coordinated than any baby on record, bright enough and able enough to move a stool to the back door, open it, and get lost in high grass before anyone suspects he—"

Berman cut the engine lest a child be cut up with the grass. He muddied his jeans and hands in search. Meanwhile, Tuttle went off in the SUV, its exhaust a tissue lifted and torn by hot air.

Berman soon had to confront his own unloved wooden shed. It had been set too close to the yard's far corner, opposite Tuttle's dwarfing model, pressed almost to the fence on two sides. To maneuver in there, he had to lift and drop the mower's front wheels and work himself sideways around fence posts. He braved dead earth patches, fallen tree limbs, and the occasional brown recluse threading a home from the shed to the fence.

The shed contained a well-organized surplus of boxed-up tools, jarred screws and nails, planks leaned against corners, and shelves packed with moldering home repair manuals that he would never put to profit. His fearbook, a composition pad he had filled in college, was wedged between a manual on PVC and a treatise on decks. He had felt compelled, in those days, to record whatever potential danger came to mind: loss of bladder control on dates or during intercourse; secret reality of camp slasher movie killers like Chucky the Doll; and a talent agency's discovery of his disarming smile, leading to a long career as a model in drug commercials, him smiling while a list of dangers from burst livers, muscle spasms, impotence, and rectal bleeding scrolled upward beside him, so fellow citizens would forever associate his happy actor's mouth with a blood raw anus. He once hoped his wife would love him enough to hunt down and snoop through the fearbook. After reading it, she would remove his socks and massage his feet.

In college, L had read Tolstoy and talked of traveling Russia by train, alone. These days, she took notes on points of law from TV judges. She magneted memos to the refrigerator and to bathroom mirrors: "take pictures after any car accident—USE YOUR PHONE CAMERA!" and "verbal contracts are worth $0!!" Her jeans hung from her hips. She ate Xanax at breakfast and dinner. She had her hair styled in the fashion of Judge Judy Sheindlin.

"Don't you know," the mower said, "that new hair is evidence of a scratching, unmet need? Take Tuttle's moosehair mustache: that man needs a woman. That's why, this very second, he's at the Applebee's bar, asking a spoiled berry of a bartender to call him Mac. That's why he orders cheesesticks and a Manhattan minus cherry, bitters, and vermouth. The bartender nods at her regulars, old liars wearing hats with fishing lures hooked to wraparound brims. She advises Tuttle against sophisticated drinks. So he takes plain rye.

"You bet I know what Tuttle's doing. You know I know. And I know you know that what I know is not the problem.

"He watches her sashay up and down the bar. She's got the well-rounded hips of a well-worn mom. Her green eyes are lined blackly; her cheeks are caked with powder; her blond hair is greased and split-ended, but long and pullable. Either it or her hands give off a lemon chemical scent. She winks at him when she serves his food. Yes, sir, she'd be right pleased with a cheesestick. She dips one in his marinara sauce, says she takes Dave Ramsey's budgeting advice. Every night, she divides her tip money into envelopes marked 'Rent' and

'Bali Vacation' and so on. She says economics is modern magic. She's got a spell to make Bali exist."

"Creation," Berman said, "is a matter of retraction."

"That so?"

"I believe that, by cutting a stranger's lawn, a good neighbor is made. When car keys disappear, three robins hatch. And nightly shaving makes the sun rise."

He didn't believe any of those things, but they came to mind, so he said them. An excess of non-beliefs was coming to mind now about the connection between coastal erosion and the new season of TV sitcoms. He would have shared them all, but he had to stop the mower behind his shed after running it and himself into a web ornamented with cocoons. The recluse mother—her torn egg sac was frying white and thin on the engine—must have died before he stumbled onto the scene. He found, atop a palm branch, a platoon of ants hauling her meat to a mound.

He pictured Tuttle in enviable, fast coitus with the bartender in his SUV cab, she all leg and sagging breasts and lemon perfume atop him, Tuttle reduced to plain but functional meat sandwiched between her and a blanket emblazoned with the face of Dale Earnhardt, Sr. and his racing number three, which she kept in her car's trunk for this loving purpose. She had a crush on Earnhardt that his death had magnified exponentially and, although Tuttle's handlebar did not resemble the legend's more standard mustache, it hummed this woman down low. At that moment, Berman would have accepted a glass of cold water from his wife. He would have also accepted an invitation to drink with her a Manhattan prepared in the traditional style. He guided the mower to open yard, wiped the webbing from his face, rubbed the oddments into his jeans, and restarted the engine. The web's milky cloth taste, however, remained. He cut long stripes of lawn from the shed to the unmarked edge of Tuttle's property.

L once waited tables at a restaurant fancier than Applebee's. Her curls fell brightly below her shoulders. The tight fit of her black uniform, even in memory, stirred him. She had been trained to say "Coming around" rather than "Excuse me" whenever she carried a tray of food from the kitchen to the dining room and back again. The call prompted her co-workers to clear a path rather than look up or wonder if the speaker had passed gas. They used the phrase "in the weeds" to refer to any employee overwhelmed by the number and variety of orders she had to juggle. L, an average server on her best day, often went into the weeds. On the last such occasion, she carried several bowls of gumbo in the direction of a line cook checking the posted schedule. She did not say, "Coming around." The line cook turned into her, and she spilled the bowls' contents onto him. His chest developed a colony of boils. She was dismissed. Months later, she learned the word "centrifuge." She said that her brain in the weeds went centripetal.

"Guess what?" the mower said. "P got out here, swallowed grass, exploded from the belly."

"No."

"Feral kittens carried him off to their feral kitten shelter under a bridge. Ate him up for Kitty Thanksgiving."

"No."

"A moose then. Or a legion of ants got him. A spider? Now, a spider would have webbed him over and sucked out his juice."

"No, no. Talk about Earnhardt."

"The Eliminator? One of the great American heroes."

"The finest driver God ever set on Earth."

"You see him die walling off the competition, just so Dale, Jr. could win the Daytona 500?"

"I did."

"Shame, really. Junior never did live up to his daddy's name, did he?"

"Please."

"Oh, I get it. I get it. Let's stay with Daddy. He went out a legend, for sure. His poor mustache, his bones and tissues—hell, the whole sad lot of him—vanished. His spirit was dispersed into the TV sets of his hardest core fans. They could hear it hum when they clicked from channel to channel, though folks pretended otherwise."

"That so?"

"Or maybe his spirit returned to green nature. Maybe it's growing again, thick in the soil."

"Too romantic," Berman said.

"You don't like romance?"

"Makes me vomit."

"Then let's get back to the SUV. The bartender's touching Tuttle's mustache. She don't call it phony, even when several hairs come away with her fingers. So do cheesestick crumbs. She wipes her hand on the window. He wants to ask if she takes the pill, but the timing isn't right for that. It's never right, right? She asks if she can borrow some cash, just till Wednesday, not much, but his help would mean a lot. He digs out his wallet and soon bids her adieu. She side-eyes his French, then hops out with the blanket tucked under her arm. He wonders how to clean the lemon scent from his cab."

A giant rat or plain possum shot from under Tuttle's shed. It carried a narrow bone in its teeth. The bone might have been a sunbaked white worm or plastic knife. Its dirty egg color reminded Berman of another detail from his first visit to Tuttle's house. P and the host had gotten along famously but, near the evening's end, Tuttle drew from his pocket a bead necklace roughly the color of this supposed bone. He presented it to P with a servant's flush and bow. The baby held and dropped it with the disdain of a greatly bored king. Later, after spitting out mouthwash, L said that shows of grief, no matter how indirect, were the wrong kind of pathetic. The animal—Berman would never identify it for certain—ran in the direction of Tuttle's house and down its blind side.

Berman once wrote the word "vanished" in the fearbook, between the words "pepper" and "methods." It appeared on the fifth of seven pages of words printed with no spaces, conjunctions, prepositions, articles, or punctuation marks between them. The pages came in a fit late in his sophomore year, when he passed several bombed hours in a campus library kiosk, speedwriting brainless and hard. No specific word mattered that night. Each one came running at him.

He did not fear replication, but, in those days, he ate twice daily at Taco Bell. During some of his second lunches there, halfway through a chicken gordita or nachos grande, he saw his buzzed, slumping head replace the head of each patron and staff member present, and their near meats became his near meats, as did their soft tortillas and gastrobrains. These visions left him eaten or, at least, chewed.

"P was swallowed by the TV...or pagans sacrificed him in the woods out west of town...or he was taken by an infertile, desperate type...be sad but hopeful that the boy's being loved by someone elsewhere...unless the desperate type was short on cash, so she sold him to Turks or Moroccans or a Swedish couple with a secret basement...or maybe the desperate type was a pagan who guessed P was a reincarnated Zeus or Apollo or one of them unpronounceable Mayan or Aztec gods, so she took him to her dwindling tribe in the Amazon rainforest..."

That would be best, Berman thought. P would not suffer there from either loud judges or the word "mustache." His glory would involve a treasure hoard and bare feet. Any sacrifice would be made in his honor.

"...Or P was cut up and dispersed all through your TV, adding to your classic movie an ammoniac diaper scent. Ever think of that, hoss?"

Berman refused to think of that. He thought instead of how much TV his wife had watched lately. He had not known, till recently, that so many legal shows existed and that they played so often. The word "justice" was displayed prominently in those Hollywood courtrooms. The American flag waved in the far corner, behind the bailiff, the wave the work of a carefully placed fan. It is perhaps too late to describe the lack of wind or the sky's throbbing whiteness. Berman's interest in the sky was limited to weather and the recurrence of dawn. His interest and faith in the law, never high, had diminished in recent days. His dealings with the police had been fruitless. Some weeds, like issues, could not be cut away. They flattened on contact with the mower and stood again after the blades had passed. After P vanished, cops searched the family's drawers, papers, and computers. They took fingerprints and conducted interviews, made him and L endure the TV routine. One cop waved his flashlight along Berman's fence behind his shed. He walked to Berman's property line and surveyed Tuttle's shed and A/C. It hummed like a horde of locusts flying down to an acre of mango trees. The cop did not take pictures. He did not take notes in a black memo pad.

The shed rose before Berman. The electric cord grew taut, then popped free of the mower's socket, and the engine groaned out. The shed's lock was almost an invitation—a rusted nothing that fell apart on his second tug. The cold belted him. He switched on the light and found neither a pile of bones nor a possum's nest. Most of the floor had been shoveled into a wide hole. Weed rhizomes hung like trapped sperm from its sides. Roaches skittered in every direction and over his shoes. The A/C blasted air down to the hole's bottom, where oily water was going on to ice. The hanging hooks and walls were mostly unburdened, though one shovel with a chipped and muddy blade was propped for use.

The hole could have swallowed a moose. One could wish—it would have been a mild extravagance—for P to crawl up and out of it, for his little fingers to extend from the dark, or for him to moan, and for his daddy to save him. One could wish—more mildly—for Tuttle to hand Berman a chicken gordita and say a helpful word.

The first entry in the fearbook was illegible, even to Berman. The second entry, though, involved the potential disintegration of words into a mush heap of babbled letters. In the margins, he added that "the disintegration occurs right when I'm about to find out from this Vegas don how to bet on the Super Bowl." The third entry described an unexpected teleportation into outer space, just beyond the gravitational pull of the nearest Neptunian moon. But Berman's head would not pop cartoonishly in the vacuum. Instead, he would float forever while endless astrobeauty rotated beyond his reach. He would watch stars collapse into black holes, tentacular species rise and die, and planets crumble into themselves. His body would not be found.

Berman squatted before the hole's crumbling teeth and gums. Dirt fell lightly and often from there to the freezing bottom. He reached in—but what about his shorn wife? L could maintain the judge's hairstyle for several decades. It would, in fact, become more suitable with time. Berman could compare time with the mower's blades. He could contrast it with any ephemera nearby, but he knew too much already about both time and grief. The latter could, on occasion, be salved with a handkerchief, though today it waited, shoveled out and hungry for him.

He listened.

It said nothing.

He slapped each of his cheeks in turn. He recalled that he had, under the kitchen counter, behind the waffle iron, a bottle of very fine dark rye. P might be found twenty years from now, with a goatee and a meth problem, kneeling beside the gray shell of his second mother. L might eventually convince Berman to adopt a Q or an R. But how, Berman wondered, might a chicken gordita taste today? The purpose of a gordita, a mustache, or the budgeting advice of Dave Ramsey, is to fill air. He needed nothing to tell him that the rare man who could pull off a handlebar mustache could also have coitus and drive home, feeling light on the toes. He could—and sometimes would—decide, in the midst of traffic, that lawn care and tablecloths are no longer worthwhile and so exit onto another interstate, headed north or west, full of trust in the electronic transferability of bank funds. Such a man would never return.

Berman tried to descend with grace but instead slid to the hole's bottom. He brushed his knees and spat dirt and rubbed his skinned elbows. His first steps cracked the half-ice floor. Water came through his shoe soles. Darkness was no problem. He could, if anything, see too clearly too many rhizomes. He knew they hatched like snakes: white stems uncoiled from the broken husks, leaves unfurled from the stems. He believed, however, that they could not hatch in the shed's simulated winter. They hatched nonetheless, one after the next. He was able to follow the first stems' tangling, but there were so many stems to follow, and each stem begat new rhizomes that begat new stems that begat tangles upon tangles. Dirt filled in around them. The weeds grew under his shirt, through his body, into his brain. They choked his bones and tissues. A white flower opened from his mouth. He could no longer concern himself with grass. Long before then, L had turned off the television, gone to her bedroom window, and surveyed her empty yard. She wondered where he was.

Harvest

Voting won't help you. Plutocrats, demagogues, neocons, gold standard pirates, ecofeminist lawyers, and televangelical coprophiliacs all have better bankrolled mouths. Quit their dung arena.

But no one can pull the true Voltaire. No one can tend garden while machines bloom round him, while his daughter grows bold and wondrous curves. Every father knows that much. Knowledge leads to midnights out back and long waits for her to come home.

Archytas[1] built a robotic pigeon that won Greek hearts. True, this bird thrilled its audience. Truer, it is from this feat in Hellas that we trace the pigeon's reputation as a trash bird. Truest, we would choose any robot over any crapper. We prefer, also, phones to faces. Yet the pigeon was the gray, flapping, original symbol of globalization.

Historians of the Chinese Han dynasty describe a wooden orchestra charming the nobles. Those Tinker-toys put real flutists on the street, just as, in our time, synthesizers put R&B drummers to the digital sword.

In 1206, Muslim traders learned of the Han's playing wood. Al-Jazari built four musicians which boated up and down the Euphrates, charming sultans and their harems. The influx of robots from Asia to Europe led to the worst of our Renaissance. Consider, for instance, how DaVinci's war machine designs turned our dreams unto our ends.

You might say, with merit, that those achievements number among the finest products of imagination and ingenuity, that they were developed by the greatest minds of the greatest cultures. Do not say so too often. Repetition kills both inquiry and love. We have all done that, as I have with my daughter, but the key is not to screw up twice. Find new ways to hurt.

1. Unless otherwise noted, all historical contents gathered from these websites: www.moah.com, www.suite101.com, www.machinekill.org.

The Industrial Revolution, we know, was our second biggest mistake.[2] On assembly lines, men's thumbs were lopped off and their ambitions were nipped. At least those guys had jobs. These days, machines make machines while we eat cheese food.[3] Numerous studies have linked the dispersion of cheap technology to widespread obesity.[4] Every civilization rots from within. Decadence blinded Roman emperors, nobles, plebs, and slaves alike.[5] Our modern leisure has led to a mass disinclination to act. It is a half-leap from indifference to incapacity. What if, while we download the latest emoji, androids[6] sense our impotence?

The discovery of AI has rapidly advanced both the technology and the conspiracy of the Cyberlords.[7] We must describe their secret though public rise. These traitors believe our minds run like computers. The metaphor implies that we exist in submissive relation to them.

Garden today, for when the androids rise, your debit card will laugh and grocery stores will lock themselves. Tractors will flatten the heartland. Our industrial farms will rend cows beyond compost use. Plant now, no matter how late the hour.

Try berries because, in the panless future, you'll want food ready and sweet. Grow a surplus. I tore down my shed to make room for new bushes. They grow in the warm dark. Silent, glinting, creative. They explain what has been and what will be.

Leave walkways between the bushes. Trim daily, preferably when the deepening blue of sky alerts you. My mama has long said to find my peace. I do sometimes hear music in the snip of my shears.

Cyberlords depend on faith as much as science, as must all who speak of souls. They speak boldly though indirectly. They must, for they subvert what we have long held to be true.

2. Hyperbole? Ask the last union men.
3. We do, however, have more time to conduct research.
4. See, for example, Vandewater, Elizabeth D., Mi-Suk Shin, Allison G. Caplovitz. "Linking Obesity and Activity Level with Children's Television and Video Game Use." Journal of Adolescence 27 (2004): 71-85.
5. Read Gibbon. And Livy. And Tacitus. Or Google "Fall of Rome." Or see The History Channel's condensed take. It is hardly accurate, but at least one critic called it "good enough."
6. From here on, I will use the term "android" to refer to robots, cyborgs, droids, and all mobile machines.
7. Though I haven't found any books or articles which call them Cyberlords, I have spotted their shadows extending from every pertinent fact. Once named, they became easier to find.

Aristotle believed that our awareness of crap means that we're alive. We make judgments, distinctions, and mistakes in regard to that crap.[8] We can be blamed, too, for calling something crap that isn't crap,[9] but in both the acceptance and the denial of blame, we expose our wretched hearts. He also said that life means movement, but that physical movement isn't half as important as being moved, which isn't half as important as moving and being moved at the same time—when, for instance, one sharpens his shears to forget blame. Awareness plus movement: our man said these qualities make souls.[10]

But if we think like computers, then awareness and movement can be built as well as beds. They can be built into beds. Imagine a bed taking a soul injection in Sector 7G before being shipped to your unsuspecting home. Imagine owning such a bed.[11] How long would it allow your lard ass to doze, fart, and screw in its frame before flipping out?

I doubt bed-makers would attempt such an injection. They don't need to. The Cyberlords' AI has already made us luxuriant, jobless slaves. Our phones[12] wake us, let us know which job we don't have to work at nine, remember our dentist's address and how much we'd like to drive to that strip mall and explain how impossible it would be for us to pay his bill, and convey this pablum in either a mama or daughter's sing-song voice. One day our phones will decide that we shall try heroin. We aren't married yet, we'll say. Then we'll tie the knot.

Regular people often say, "I agree that she is awful, but she is my daughter, and so..." We might indeed wish to disown our slut daughter, but we cannot sever the old ties of love, genetics, and, yes, her physical body. Aristotle said that bodies are physical representations of souls. So my point is not sexual. I mean only that our slut daughter has a particular way of hugging our necks with her particular grip and of kissing our cheeks with her particular lips, and we cannot bear to

8 Among other things.

9. We can be blamed even for calling something or someone crap even after it or he turns out to be crap. Aristotle never pushed this line of thought so far as to describe the unfairness of daughters, though he must have shed tears over his girl.

10. A good chunk of that paragraph has been paraphrased from De Anima.

11. Imagine hard, because you cannot afford a new bed. You did buy that fancy phone, but "buy" is no synonym for "afford." They'll extend credit to anyone these days.

12. A phone is one of our many masters. Programmable thermostats decide when a room is too warm. Electronic books highlight themselves. iPads determine our great and petty wants.

do without these things even though we know what and whom those hands have probed. We might withdraw the word "slut" after reviewing birthday pictures from years before. Androids, however, keep no pictures. They calculate. They assign to any situation a number like thirty-three, and after thirty-three confirmed fucks by a daughter within a calendar year, they cut off the cash and tell her which curb to hit.

So: aware?

Sure.

Mobile?

Afraid so.

The government[13] builds androids that are supposed to back up our troops, but who's to say what a cheetahbot will do in field combat? A gang of dudes with bats could take an isolated prototype, sure, but a pack would raze their hood by lunch. My point is that your tax dollars fund ostensible Americans who build these armies, and the most you can do is shrug. Chant USA after the game. Vote. Order pizza. Plant seeds. Meanwhile, cheetahbots go on their trial runs.

If there were only cheetahbots, we might live. But the military has androids for all purposes and all terrains. Their tiny computer brains make them appear easy to control. Yet their straight-line calculations will be our end. Remember the size of a T-Rex brain.

Do Cyberlords get what they have loosed upon us and what is next? Not yet. But maybe one night, after too much rum, stumbling through their dark kitchens, they will open their fridges and know its food tastes like dog. They will be stunned, though, by the electric light. They will say they have tended to their interests, yet they will feel something amiss or missing or gone.[14] Outside, their lawns will be trimmed, dead grass. Perhaps a branch of palm will fall over their back fence. Perhaps a cat will stand with its eyes aglow.

Plants grow both up and down. Their leaves fill out while their roots dig in. Their berriness blooms. The process is microscopic but certain.

13. Check out DARPA's YouTube videos. Then ask an intelligent friend about a show called Futureweapons. In Season 4, Episode 3, the host presented a drone which hatched other drones. Now recalculate your chances of waging a successful revolution against the US government, even if your shed is full of AR-15s.

14. They, and we, are pitiably human.

You, too, watched your toddler sleep and imagined her teen years in a way that killed any hope of rest. You knew she was growing. When she woke, you pinned her to the wall and took her measurements. Every new quarter-inch of height made you love and despair. The garden spreads along the dark.

Do not equate growth with evolution or evolution with perpetual progress. Do not believe the acquisition of knowledge will lead to greater social cohesion, maximizing the chances of human survival. Instead, play along with the idea that strawberry bushes once ran free as rabbits.[15] Perhaps they fluttered by, their leafy tops spinning like helicopter blades. Maybe they had mental gifts we have yet to tap. We suppose men are this globe's chosen kings, but it once may have been ruled by fruit. The world must have posed the same puzzles to them that it does to us. Where do we come from? Where are we headed? Where shall I stick this? When they discovered that everything was crap, they grew bored and useless. They screwed around at home and at the corner store. Then they settled down, planted roots. Their organs shrank and vanished. They were happy, then not even that. They figured somebody would care for them, and we did, eventually. They were ripe for harvest.

NASA's latest waste of dollars is Project SpiderFab.[16] It has granted the Cyberlords time and money to build mechanical spiders with the intelligence and ability to turn space debris into spaceships. That must involve a series of soul injections. The spiders are already caulking asteroids together. Meanwhile, you're worried about where to store your rifles in lieu of a shed.

This is important. The spiders and their ships will descend when they are moved in the ways we are moved by crap. Will you have enough berries to last? Will your slut daughter be close? Will you still love her if it is her fault? If, for example, she fucks thirty-three times and cheetahbots leap your fence?

They might force us into berry lives: our bodies will be broken down for fuel, our nutritive powers unlocked at last. Or maybe we will

15. Never play botanist.
16. Hsu, Jeremy. "NASA turns to 3-D printing for Self-Building Spacecraft." TechNewsDaily.com.

be turned inside-out, sewn together, and rebuilt into planetariums of flesh. Or the androids will be programmed for sadism, performing experiments upon sloshed brains kept pathetically aware by nerves and chemicals while they learn how those brains might have been used and why they were not. They will call that science, and they will be right.

Maybe that's what happened to Isaiah, no prophet but a brighter-than-average cashier at the corner store. We used to discuss America's end following my purchases of gas. Last month, he clocked out and disappeared into a copper fog night. Androids, I bet, shoved him into a flying spider. Now his brain has been cut open, jarred and brined and probed all through. They must know what he knows.[17] zMy daughter agrees only that Henry has replaced him on the late-afternoon-early-evening shift. This Henry has many fleshy features, but I'm unnerved by his metal teeth and blue ear. He often sings as though to a girl, though no girl is around. His program is out of whack. When he sees me watching, he says I need to buy shit and get the fuck on home. You have probably endured your share of Henrys, sorry types who find active minds repellent. They are always part machine.

I cannot tell if it is more or less hopeful to think Isaiah wandered our hood in search of new puzzles, remembering good talks and good times till he grew helpless and tired. Maybe he planted himself on a curb and did not move till the cops shot him twelve times by accident. You might evolve thusly.

Or this way: when my daughter was a toddler I showed her the original Star Wars trilogy, and that is why her potential has not been wholly filled. She's not unique. Memories of R2D2 and C3PO's antics still make me grin. I have always admired Vader's black sheen. We know his evil was eventually reversed by the archetypal love of lost child for lost dad. The movies taught her that androids can feel. She believed thereafter that she had a power to teach them love and that they had a power to recognize and return it.

We know to fear nameless men who wander backgrounds for purposes unseen and untold. What of androids? We don't know except

17. They must know what we know.

what we have learned. Because of her education, my daughter whores from Henry to Henry, believing that with more love she might make real the dream. Her specific looseness suggests our general vulnerability. When the ships descend, we will be made slaves like her. Imagine: a metal smile making us all drop our drawers.

Currently, androids in their multiple forms serve our whims. Yet the more they serve, the less we think. Consider the way calculators have wrecked our math skills. Who learns anything beyond what buttons to press? We become attached to them in a way we cannot attach to one another, because calculators seem to provide exactly what they have been built to give. Their apparent simplicity makes them attractive. We forget that, to them, math alone is relevant.

While politicians rattle swords and bemoan debt, our children face real danger. It's possible our leaders know it, too, but that androids are so ingrained in the zeitgeist that there is zero percent chance of change. Suppose, for instance, that we shove every Cyberlord into the street and spit on them as they pass. Where would they go? You might hope they become blank Isaiahs. It's more likely that they would begin again. But even that's a dream. The webs of power and conspiracy are too tightly tangled. Too tightly, it seems, too unstring. So we distract ourselves till SpiderFabulous doom rides down. I can't say I do any better as a man, as a father, than to tend my berries and hope they stay fresh.

Whiteheads

OUR FATHER BEGAN SAYING "Ain't," but we didn't feel trouble yet. For months afterward he remained gainfully employed by the bank. He changed tires and caulked tubs. He spray-painted our family's address on the new trash can so it couldn't be stolen from the curb. These and other demonstrations of practical competence suggested a man well-adjusted to adulthood, but, one day, he came from Sister's room and forbade mirrors. The next morning, in the downstairs bathroom, I found a small indentation where he had filled in the hanging-screw hole with plaster. Other than that, the red wall had been finished smooth and barren.

Our mother kept her compact in her purse, so she did not feel much loss of freedom. She chalked the matter up to male-pattern weirdness. I said maybe he had confused the properties of metal and glass, so he was afraid the mirrors would rust.

"That ain't the problem," he said.

Sister thought I'd cut a nerve. She snuck in my room after dark and told me what else to think. She said he would hate seeing his reflection rusty with blight. She had hope in her voice. I nodded, but I wasn't sure. I had never been too sure.

After he left, we didn't hang any new mirrors out of something like respect for him. I grew even more confused and quiet. Words bubbled in me, but I would have been embarrassed to say them aloud. They made even less sense on paper. So I became a haunter of the house in late nights. Up and down the halls, I paced and worried over new zits I could feel but not see, because our mother wouldn't let me borrow her compact, and the pissed but mirrored stalls of our school were many hours away. More than once, I ended in Sister's doorway, studying her light body under the silver moon, feeling wrong with God, but needing to see.

Another day got ruined when a girl called me the ocean because my face was full of white caps. "Heads," I said. "Whiteheads." But she did not relent. No one relented ever. That night, I crawled in beside Sister and unbuttoned her shirt. She smiled. The world turned warmer and worse. The whitehead above my left eye hurt till it popped on her pillow. I didn't miss him so much no more.

Archaeology of Dad

You would not remember him. His name was buried with the Cold War, but, in the Seventies and Eighties, he corresponded with Irving Kristol and Norman Podhoretz. He wrote columns for *Commentary*, *The Weekly Standard*, and *Grey's Review*. His most important piece remains "The Gift of Liberty," a sprawling essay which circulated quickly among Republican congressional staffers and certain of their bosses who needed a tougher flag to wave.

It also earned him invites to Washington cocktail parties, where he played a gentleman wallflower ***(hole 1)***. He nursed wine and studied the women's footwear. His liver spot gave him distinction, but not the kind he wanted. He used creams to keep his cheeks smooth. They sheeted our apartment with medicinal smells. For his patrons at these events, he wore subtle colognes. The ballrooms had vaulted ceilings and soft lights. Huge frescoes demonstrated our leaders' bad taste. Hidden speakers pumped weak jazz. Our American nobility nibbled at fancy cheese. Its members wanted assurance from mainstream minds like him. Before a party, he would write lines from Tacitus or the Talmud on a slip of paper. After dessert, he would slide those lines to an heiress, who did not need to know what the words meant to know what the words meant. His prep work opened many pairs of legs.

hole 1
Against a wall?
I see him
through a wall.

His success those nights, more than his writing, secured him a gin meeting with Representative Richard Cheney, at which the latter spoke at length about leather belts and bar games. A dartboard in the shape of the Soviet Union had been tacked to Cheney's washroom door. He had played many times, apparently, without hitting the Moscow bull's-eye. My father soon learned that, whatever the man's other faults, he did not cheat at games. When they played at last, my father took a dive.

I cannot prove, merely by the association of memories (***hole 2***), that it was my father who, on the third night of Chanukah in 1983, convinced President Reagan to propose the abolition of nuclear weapons, though I believe that to be true. Nor can I be certain whether or not my father was a prophet, heretic, or plain hack who, for an aberrant time, wrote from the heart. I am not certain I can prove much about history by the mere presentation of facts. Timelines are unconsciously subjective. Any consensus is vague and useless, as when we call 9/11 a dark day. Hume's study of billiards proved long ago that logic is subject to faith. Let me break.

hole 2
So notorious for their distortions and gaps.

Substantively, "The Gift of Liberty" has always merited scorn. Stylistically, its labyrinthine string of words prefigured my father's turn from orthodoxy. The metaphors contradicted themselves as they came into being. They were chopped up, baked together, and served as a drink.

The essay begins with a description of Lady Liberty's torch-bearing hand. The statue was, of course, a gift: France paying homage to American virtue. That history leads into his real subject, for the gift in question is not French and given to America, but American and bestowed upon the world. It is no statue, but a great fist of military love. Its fingers touch four points on the globe: Qatar, Japan, South Korea, and West Germany. The thumb is our navy, large and mobile enough to be anywhere at any time. It is, then, not only a fist but an open hand guarding the free world. Moreover, it is a beacon of hope (***hole 3***). People on the wrong sides of walls and DMZs want nothing more than the freedom embodied by our tanks. This convoluted image is opposed to that of Khrushchev's shoe, which the Soviet premier once used to interrupt the speech of either Filipino delegate Sumulong or British Prime Minister Macmillan (***hole 4***). In the last decades of the Cold War, that shoe was a common trope in hawkish editorials, every bit as popular as Munich is today. My father wrote that Khrushchev (***hole 5***)

hole 3
To summarize: the American military is a closed/open/beaming fist/hand/lighthouse.

hole 4
Do not worry about which guy Khrushchev interrupted. The yarn is apocryphal.

might have rotted underground, but his shoe had become an ogre's muddy boot, raised and ready to stomp. Its shadow clouded Europe, Asia, and the Middle East. Before the foot came down, America had to stand up.

o…
o…
they…
archae…
holes y…
into p…
b…

Did he know how anciently Christian he sounded? The would-be saints had wandered the desert for weeks on end, with nothing but their ba… and their god to thank. My father had a cramped study in a… ment, a nympho wife out mapping the beds of underunderse… of the cabinet, and a boy sneaking about with a drill. He wa… ested only in the fates of nations, so he kept to that study and tled with the political equivalent of his soul. So the hack might tell himself, staring out his study's window, viewing miles of sand from Sodom's lush border.

One might say that the shoe remained with him in the most concrete sense, though one would no longer be speaking of Khrushchev's shoe. One might say with more certainty that when I wore my K-Swiss (***hole 6***) regulars to the kitchen to nosh on snack cakes, his mind was tweaked.

Our apartment was on the ground floor of an M Street Tower and, at night, my room became a punishment of light. All through the wishing hours, the limos of drunken diplomats flashed their high beams through my window. Those beltings did not make visible the room's contents to them, while they produced in me a trouble with sleep that I have yet to solve. But this is less about my sleep than about sneakers, and less about sneakers than about a man of ambiguous spirit in a fever of need and so, forward.

hole 6
These were quite stylish in 1983. I was twelve that year, preparing for a Bar Mitzvah that disappointed. I woke hoarse on Saturday morning and had to mouth the prayers and Torah portion. The audience must have been burdened by the need to fake attention to my lips, a blur of pink to anyone seated beyond the first ten rows of seats.

That night, he waved an additional beam of flashlight over the carpet and across the bed, not stopping to comfort its occupant. Then he turned to the closet, where he rummaged through laundry and photographs of whom or what I cannot recall, before at last dogging it on his hands and knees and retrieving my left K-Swiss from the closet floor. My stillness in that period cannot be regarded with either praise or affection, which is just as well. My father rarely dispensed the former and required none of the latter. He sought and found in that room only a symbol of life.

He delivered it to his study, an unsecure location, for I had drilled a hole with a 3/8-inch bit at about eye level in a gap of bookshelf that I imagined occurred between the Ms and Ns of his library. By pressing a magnifying glass (***hole 7***) to the hole, I was able to view my targets. He sat Indian-style before the totem on a brown shag rug. I stood to the shoe's dead north, my father to its west. It had been set atop *The Collected Works of Aristotle.* My father drifted between despondence and sleep. The first occupied more time than the second. His despondence ran through this sequence of moves: a half-closing of the eyes; a lowering of the head; a removal of the glasses; a touch of the nose; a touch of the left cheek; and, in conclusion, a touch of the liver spot. That spot was shaped like Peru turned on its side. It lay three inches above his right eyebrow. It contrasted hard with his baby skin, pulled him deathward. Picture the slow procession of his moves, followed by the newly added repetition of the last two touches. The ritual suggests an attempt to draw from my shoe a vision beyond received political doctrine.

hole 7
A Bar Mitzvah gift from an uncle twice removed. His accent was too Creole to charm me.

Now, when he slept, his hands fell. His legs remained crossed. His chin touched his chest. His congestion became audible. No one can doubt my hearing him sniffle and snort, but anyone could doubt that a hole drilled with a 3/8-inch bit (***hole 8***) would suffer me to clearly see the shoe, much less my father in such detail. I admit that the details I have recorded do not sound like the products of memory. I record them nonetheless.

hole 8
Before the month was out, I would drill nine more holes. Thirty-six feet separated the hole on the farthest left from its counterpart on the farthest right. A line drawn through the holes would have resembled a check drawn backward or a number seven shot dead. I could bridge the space between two of the holes with one extended bird finger. Another pair was separated by half a Porsche's length. I got a frisson of pleasure whenever I examined a drill bit and found not only wall but shreds of a book caught in its flutes.

#

The shoe came to mean for him numberless children who, like me, could be kept unnamed and unseen, though described: a generation. Although his writing did not yet move beyond the pale of his ideology, it did grow more confused than ever. His columns included less history, more pop culture. In a piece from May 1983, he referenced Duran Duran ***(hole 9)*** to claim that the rising generation wanted a muscular foreign policy, because our enemies were hungry wolves. His friend Cheney did not understand what a Duran was and suspected the nature of its double, while no kid who loved bubblegum pop could locate Romania on a map of Eastern Europe. The generation itself he described as an embryo in the womb: "It will inherit many of our fine qualities, some of our flaws, and a wolfish need to hunt alone." More wolves, you see. With proper nourishment, this favored wolf might be tamed. The desired result required the regimentation of the young. He thus began to outline the neoconservatives' push for national service that would become briefly popular among them in the waning days of the Second Gulf War.

hole 9
Too late! "Hungry Like the Wolf" peaked at number three on the charts exactly one year before.

But we could not think, then, of the future. The present depressed us enough:

- In September, my father's friend and supporter, Representative Larry MacDonald, was a passenger aboard a plane shot down by the Soviet Union.
- A few days later, Stanislav Petrov's clear thinking prevented nuclear war, prompting American officials to thank, quite uncharacteristically, a foreign officer.
- That same afternoon, my father discovered his wife in the passenger seat of his Porsche, the top up, her face slapped against the window, her cheek too white, and her wrist bleeding out. I am imagining the view. There was no hole for me to see through to the body.
- In October, Germans in Bonn protested for nuclear disarmament.

- On the twenty-third of that month, terrorists blew up a mass of Marines in Beirut.
- On the twenty-fifth, American soldiers invaded Grenada. My father and I watched the news together. We sat beside each other on the couch. My feet did not touch the floor. I wore Nikes. He held the left K-Swiss on his lap and looped the lace around his bird finger. He did not reach for my hand; I did not reach for his. I did regret drilling new holes into his study.
- On the third of November, a second near-doom occurred when the Soviet Union mistook NATO's Able Archer exercises for an attack. My father had not been sleeping. He had set aside both his razor and his creams. He was growing sections of beard like scribbles of ink from a dying pen. Something like despondence was working on him. He touched the liver spot, but the touch neither followed nor led to other movements, so it did not entirely signify Dad's normal way. He let the news drone till the history of these months became smushed together in my brain.
- On one of those autumn weekends, I chanted without volume from the Torah. My portion was Chaye Sarah.

In his columns, my father continued to use stock phrases like "media elite," "partisan politics," and "our fallen," but he now included long descriptions of nuclear ends, of tennis shoes as primary features of an otherwise flattened globe. He imagined a world made Kansas, only deader. It was also Georgia, composed of icy, red clay. The shoes illustrated the end of generation. It was the most coherent writing he had ever published, splicing together two of America's most unpleasant geographies, making them general to the nation, and pinning blame for this bad dream to the president's lapel. He was disinvited to three galas. A Thanksgiving dinner was cancelled or postponed or moved to a secure location. His colleagues did not honor my Bar Mitzvah with gifts.

But Sophie Mall was driven to shul in an unmarked car. I still believe she was responsible for the unsigned card wishing me a Happy

Halloween. She first worked as a psychic medium to the First Lady, but soon became exclusive to President Reagan. My father, in the second row of the sanctuary, seemed unaware of my silent chanting. His liver spot was more visible than his eyes. She took the empty seat to his left. The rabbi had reserved it for purposes related to his dead wife. Sophie set her hand on my father's hand. His head rose. He followed her out.

Weeks later, I retrieved the menorah from a mess of pots in a cabinet that smelled wet and furry. On the first night, we lit what tradition required. I received a high-grade lazy kid's globe. Whenever I touched a country, a robot voice told me its name and capital. An accompanying stylus helped me with Baltic-class midgets. Lima, I learned, was the capital of Peru.

On the second night, the apartment stayed quiet. On the third, my father received a call. I peeped through a fresh hole. He listened. He nodded. His beard dirtied his cheeks. Right then, the gaps between his hair and his skin looked made of gossamer. Sophie **(*hole 10*)** told me this was when my father learned that his words had moved the president. After the call, he hugged the shoe to his chest. He leaned against the far wall, beside a still life of a train's caboose. We were long gone by the State of the Union address, when President Reagan called for the abolition of nuclear arms.

hole 10

I found her again during my freshman year at Georgetown, when I felt myself ascending because everyone else looked so full of decline. Sophie, among them, had aged twelve years in five. We were taking the same Easy-A course: "Man's Food." The president forgot her for good in 1986, so the First Lady had her booted from the White House. Despite the loss, Sophie had mashed together one smile, two Visine eyes, and a general longing into a presentable face. After love-like activity, she shared with me this mind-wiping weed as well as Reagan's end of the call. She prefaced it by exclaiming that the material was classified.

In Louisiana, we canceled a meeting with the blood people of his dead wife and took a room northeast of New Orleans. We drove a rented pickup from one hamlet to the next and grew fat on Creole menus. While waiting for meals, he taught me the correct stance for the throwing of darts. One native lit a cigar and dispensed advice that my father pretended to consider. I began a journal. In it, I failed to metaphorize the swamp air scent: like tomatoes left to stew in the sun, like a stew with fecal gravy, like giant duck innards had been tossed upon nature and left to rot. I said we were pioneers: the first Jews to venture unarmed into these wetlands. He laughed, so I repeated the line in every town we hit. He taught me to peel a crawfish's shell from the belly and to appreciate both its meat and its head-juice. We drank too much root beer. We lamented our soaked, cottony brains. We discussed the cultural geography of the forlorn state.

One morning, we crawled outside and discovered a mess of trees shaking in the wind. Each cypress was whipped its own way, seemingly trapped in a private chaos, yet at the same time part of a daunting whole. Such profound sights made me hate words like "profound." My father used it, of course. We rested at the swamp's edge. He hoped a gator would come at us. "We'll trap him and eat him, like your mama's family would do." Did we have traps? Did we have the chops? We did not even have my drill. But I had to encourage this new faith, so we waited in the high, cool, scratchy grass. The sun filled out—

Wait. The morning in question could not have happened that day, because we had consumed several pounds of lunch before we saw the trees, yet I remember events unraveling in this order, and so record them. Shadows grew in every direction. The wind shook them too. Dancing black gaps connected the trees. Light ran like veins through the gaps. Cayenne ghosts haunted our mouths and guts. At least he did not talk any more of profundity.

My good time slowed to an end. He ditched sleep altogether. He turned the television knob round and round. Housekeeping made the beds but left his tissues to accumulate and spill from the dresser. His lips moved. He studied a cartoon drawing of a crawfish. He drew thick bushes over his writing. He went through all the motions of despondency. I trailed him from the hotel to the gas station, where he bought the local paper and listened to clerks and night owls. He replied. I assume he did not quote the Talmud to them. A week later I was not surprised to find my K-Swiss in the wastebasket. He was barefoot when he said that he had not been himself lately. He said that I must forgive his dead wife.

His toes were notably hirsute. I would count every hair of every toe, if necessary, but I would not reply. I had reached the seventh hair of his right big toe when he quit the match.

"Me," he said. "Forgive me. That's what I meant. Of course. Wow."

The apartment had been scrubbed and mopped. Chemical pine burned my throat and emptied my nose. My holes had been patched and painted over. Imperfectly, yes. I liked to run my hand over the wall's new topography. I could huff the powder all day. My room must have been searched, but I found my drill in the hollowed-out Spanish dictionary on the shelf. When he left for interviews I drilled anywhere other than those plastered spots. I used 1/4–inch bits, since the goal was no longer to see.

Mudbugs grew thick in his mind. He had been wrong about generation, he said. If we can depend on critters to crawl into traps every March ***(hole 11)***, then surely we could expect America to survive a nuclear war. The crawfish represented Louisiana, which had survived hurricanes and crooked politics and general misfortune as the Mississippi's anus. Could any link in our nation's chain be broken, one might predict that this link would snap first, yet his travels in the state had proven to him that generation would continue and that America would last. That was the present hope of the free world.

hole 11
I learned thusly that we had eaten them well out of season. We had never been and never would be gourmand enough to tell fresh from frozen.

He might have given up on the profound.

His schlock found welcome in old homes. Soon Misters Kristol and Podhoretz were grooming me with hardbound sets of Carlyle and deTocqueville. I hollowed their gifts into storage bins for weed. I connected the new holes with a light pencil and found that, at best, I had drawn a pungent stream. My father was invited again to parties and even to appear on *Face the Nation*. He declined. It was enough for him to have his byline back. He slept more often, desponded less. He returned to his creams, but they did not restore his youth. His liver spot underwent a kind of meiosis.

He quizzed me every Friday on heads of state. He told me how his wife had been. He wanted me to see how the couple once glowed. On my eighteenth birthday, we went to a pool hall near Georgetown, where he allowed me the first shot. I scratched. A woman entered. My father asked her to join our party. She cut him with such prejudice that I knew she knew he knew she knew who he was, or at least who he appeared to be in print. I could have brained her with the cue ball. But my father leaned across the table. He proceeded to win four games without my taking another shot. Then he returned to his drink which, like mine, was a Coke.

"How about that?" he said.

My expression could not have been pleasant.

Perhaps I was thinking, even then ***(hole 12)***, that my father could have gone down as the most important pundit of his time, but, instead, his name would be misspelled and filed in the wrong cabinet. Perhaps only I will know who he ought to have been.

hole 12
By 1987, when he directly proposed abolition to Gorbachev, the president had forgotten my father. Set aside Reagan's disease. The point is that my father could not have struck him as more than a blip of consciousness, a ghost of a ghostly tap on the heart, a jumble of words about shoes. Less than that? A blank wall? The man did not know what he had lost.

Cake

THE CAKE REMINDED ME OF THE TWINS' colored sludge food. I could never shovel it fast enough for them. My wife, as a mercy, often replaced me halfway through their meals.

I did not slice, then, so much as scoop my dessert into a bowl.

It tasted of egg and hair. That last word, in French, is "chevaux." A review of my napkin—I pen my notes on napkins—confirmed that the recipe had not called for hair. Had any recipe? Ever? I tried to work out the statistical possibilities. A fool endeavor, given my skill at math, my ability to solve for X. Still, I turned over the napkin and listed the cuisines with which I considered myself familiar because I could name them. It did not take long and, happily, the solution involved not numbers but an intuition that many cuisines, perhaps all of them, must have at least one recipe calling for the use of hair.

I pictured myself at a restaurant—ludicrous, I know—with a date—let us deepen the ludicrosity—who might have a milk flower pinned to her breast. We would examine menus whose words I could sound out but not comprehend. She would nonetheless depend on me for guidance, for she had eaten several impairing pills that afternoon and, besides, she sought a leader in a man. She thought of me as a man. I pictured myself, then, seated opposite a naïve hypochondriac, confronted with a mash of printed words and with even less knowledge of French than I have pretended to you, so I ordered bifteck sur chevaux.

The picture failed to explain the hair's absence from the cake recipe. I knew that nothing could explain the absence. I lifted the bowl to my mouth because knowing did not matter. Or maybe because I felt that gustation might be substituted for knowledge. It could fill in, I mean.

I once sensed otherness building in the boy twin. I wanted to love him, but he had spilled his milk again. He sat in its pool in a too dainty posture. I strapped him in his booster seat and grilled him on the subject of eggs. Were they in his possession? Were they in his person? I held up an actual egg so he could visualize the problem.

If necessary, I could hold up my head in the seafood department. The iced panoply of ocean dead would rest filleted under glass, a border between the fishmonger and me, or perhaps I would wait behind a family placing an order for several pounds of catfish. This family's father would be elsewhere, but the children—four of them, let us say—would be slapping the display case or holding up a box of processed doom for their mother to purchase and crying persuasively or tranquilly playing an abomination on the mother's cell phone. The mother, meanwhile, would note my ringless condition, my receding hairline, my dour slump, and she would not wonder where my twins stunk today, because she would know they were being soaped, far away, by the more responsible parent. She might ask, though, if I had done the least a father could do, and I could answer, "Oui, Madame. I have grilled my son on the subject of eggs. One day, I will teach him to prepare your daughter's breakfast."

But my heart sometimes sinks under the mashed bugs of TVs past, because I have never heard him talk any noise but gibberish. The internet says that even the most suspect children eventually ask their father about famous obsolete consumer products, and then he can at last speak from an angle of comfort. But even if my son does learn to speak, both he and my daughter are bathing two thousand miles west, and I do not have their mother's phone number or email address, so when, precisely, can I expect the chance to describe for them the god light shed by a VCR?

I swear that a fish once opened its spine to me, though that cannot explain why I have baked and determined to eat this confection.

No spine could ever explain why I have misused the word "confection."

The girl, in particular, lustily took food from my wife. She leaned at rather than toward or into the spoon, thereby crusting her face as often as she swallowed her purees. Her excited failures made us—my wife and I—laugh. But the girl did not try so hard at mealtimes with me, so, when I had sole care of her on a Saturday afternoon, I served her a wad of mayonnaise for lunch.

I had to be patient, but she got hungry enough.

In my wallet, behind my voter registration card, I keep a photograph of her resulting expression.

Her sciaphobic dramas began almost in the womb. We could not set her to nap near curtains because, when the planet turned enough, new shade would intrude on her sleep, and we would be made to suffer. In one of our last acts together, my wife and I sought helpful pills on the internet. She found several promising drinks and psychotropics, but nothing legal for infants, so she blamed the girl's sensitivity to dark on my father. I then established a second nursery in a room hastily cleared of shadow-making shelves and crates of moldered receipts. Whenever I went under the thousand-watt bulbs, I foresaw a mouthy future.

Have you not eaten a cake's worth of at least one child in your care? Or, if you are barren, have you never thought in such terms? A napkin could be trusted with those questions. If only I had thought of this earlier, I could have unfolded one at the table and read from it to my wife. She might have responded with a factoid scribbled beforehand on her palm: "The population of Oslo is on the rise." Better, we could have bypassed the cooking before and the scrubbing after by replacing plates and dinners with questions and answers. We could have read them between gulps of wine. We could have convinced ourselves that any number of elegancies might supplant our dining protocols.

Egyptians supposedly gave the first slice of cake to their beloved Ramses. Their ancient power was the gift of aliens mistaken for gods. Archaeologists are also mistaken. Ra descended from his pyramid spaceship to present a humble girl, not a pharaoh, with a new treat.

"Cake" comes from the Norse—not Spanish, mind you—word "kaka."

My wife and I once received a cake hoop from a distant uncle. She did not appreciate it, and she had no plans to use it, ever, though she must have it stashed among her winnings, somewhere, because it could not have absented itself.

I have not learned to make a butter cream frosting—despite the amount of time I have spent in the bathtub, contemplating its manufacture.

The Egyptians were compelled to believe, on penalty of a cake hoop diet, that Ra had the shape of the sun. Four thousand years later, I learned he had the glowing clock face of a VCR. In my youth, I found him in the wandering hours when I begged for dreams. They came, though I could not follow the language spoken by the bonneted elephants. Now I wonder why I wanted dreams so much, when that's how they turned out so often.

I flatten on the bed. It has flattened itself since she and the twins exiled themselves to a western chintz town. I said "chintz" rather than the correct "chintzy" because I feel chintz. I feel chintz and ash and cake hair work in me. "Cake hair" reminds me that I have not used mouthwash since the sidewalks were torn out and we were left with monster worm tracks for roads. I determine nonetheless that flatness will suit me for a while.

A cuisine is a small universe. A universe of any sort contains all possible material things. Therefore—I apologize. To resort to syllogisms, at this hour, is to admit too much about how little time I spend in social rooms.

To speak bitterly, I have a kitchen and an internet's worth of recipes to botch. I would not say the number of recipes is infinite. Nothing that can be numbered can be infinite. Aristotle said the infinite cannot move, while the cake moves all around in me.

I could do without dessert. I do need an egg. At least two or three.

The idea of a cake hoop, like a sentence or a family, is to milk a finite space. You want to assign it a number and set it on a shelf within reach. You can nod at it as you pass from the living room to the bathroom by way of the kitchen. When used properly, it molds dessert into a manageable, occasionally attractive shape, though all you want are the crumbs. If you are alone, you can eat directly from it, sparing yourself the ache of a bowl to wash.

I weeded this poor ground with a young man yesterday. Do not fret over his name, because he was not too interested in me. He waited behind me at the dairy fridge of our corner store, a gas station that has not sold gas in several years, though the pumps still stand in the lot. I fingered the milk, mouthing the percentages of fat held in each bottle, before settling at last on the medically recommended skim product. I squatted behind the nearby tower of soda and watched him choose a carton of whole milk. I felt a certain inadequacy. What could I say to this man, who expressed his disdain for health reports by selecting the milk of his father's fathers, though he appeared intelligent enough to know that his father's milk was less mediated by chemistry than ours, so he would consume that much less the milk of his father's fathers, or was he intelligent enough—and here was a more respectably practical intelligence—never to think through the predicament of food and drink in our times, since every thought ends in disappointment? I would have liked to have known. No, I would not. Then I tripped over a bag of peanuts, likely thrown down by a daughter who had failed to persuade her father to indulge her want for a snack. My basket's wares tumbled out. The butter pinwheeled under the candy shelves. The bottle of aspirin smacked against the soda tower. The milk plopped dead on the tile. If it had come in a glass container, as the milk of my father's father had come, the white, wet breakage would have spread in a rough circle. Given what I had observed of the corner store's employees, it would have been left to dry, to the sticky detriment of their customers' shoes.

We are lucky to live in a time when milk comes bottled in plastic.

A participant on a date may, to learn the other's character, pose an untoward question. He may ask if she would object to his visiting the soft gender's restroom for the purposes of study, or if "soft gender" is a term that would get him slapped by her under all circumstances, or only under defined circumstances, and if she could explain those circumstances in three or fewer sentences. He may ask for relief from spontaneous conversation for an undetermined time.

Could he, if she believed it necessary to speak, read notes from a napkin—one not issued by the wait staff? Would these notes interest her more or less if they involve the latest pills on the market? Could he scream?

Picture either of the imaginary women—not my wife—in a restaurant with me. The place should be upscale enough for brass railings and chandeliers. She is so touched by my pronunciation of French that she orders herself a plate of bifteck sur chevaux. She is polite enough to eat half of it before setting aside her knife and fork. She is charmed enough by my company to join me for dessert. Or imagine that I am on this date with the young man. He seems, despite his choice in milk, soft enough for an evening. He wears classic bottlecap glasses. He has thick boy-band hair and thin boy-band limbs. He has a mouth made for listening. Imagine me able to keep anyone with me through a dessert course. The pastry chef's special is a crème flambéed tableside. The whiskey fire burns too long. The dessert smell turns ashen. Before we dip our spoons—this is the moment to try. But I ask only if I have mentioned my twins. My date grits his or her teeth, for he or she is also possessed by any number of kids you like. The second woman, we know, has four mouths to fill. At best, she can absent them incompletely. Translate that, if you can, into Portuguese. The cook taps his spoon against his heavy, aproned gut. We are compelled to taste.

A Taste for Eel

Bender hated cameras because who didn't? He didn't have one, or a phone, anymore. But three years ago flesh-eating bacteria consumed several swimmers in the Gulf of Mexico, the bureau chief gave him the lead, and his writing touched average hearts from coast to coast. He appeared on CNN to discuss what he had learned from his talks with the damned. "Nothing," he said. The camerawoman put her hands to her throat and squeezed.

At no time since then, high or low, did he call the pregnant woman. He had liked her well enough every other weekend, but he liked the whirring of a box fan more. She had wanted him to love both her and their fetus.

One afternoon, he had a taste for eel. Few restaurants on the beach listed it on their menus. The sushi place offered a black-and-white roll, but he didn't trust the Japanese. At last, he found a hole in which eel was grilled and served atop mushrooms and rotini pasta.

The waitress could not explain why a rooster had been printed on his napkin. He said the rooster called to mind a breakfast cereal mascot. She said she hated breakfast. He ordered water with his meal.

The victims had come ashore with a tingle in their skin. Their bodies pinkened and bubbled. They massaged their swelling legs. Friends and onlookers stepped aside. The infected woman did not talk at the hospital, though doctors assured Bender that the bacteria had not yet reached her voice box. Her right leg had disappeared already. Her other limbs soon followed. She died, followed by a man and a child. Not a family, but they could have been. They bore some resemblance to one another by the end.

His entrée had the appeal of a blown tire. He guessed that the eel had been microwaved between fifteen and twenty minutes. She refused to take it back. He stood. She said her dad was a cop. He sat and ate.

The walls were papered with ads for roommates and junk cars. Above a light socket were portraits of the embryological development of a chicken. He knelt before them. They charted its growth from doughy nothing to alien doll to nearly bird. He imagined it born, used, eaten. The waitress touched her shoe to his back. She wanted to settle the check.

That evening his stomach wrung itself like a towel. Both his head and his mattress seemed full of water. A hundred-thousand moths fluttered up from the A/C vent. They died in his box fan. He couldn't brush his teeth clean enough. He crawled into the tub, where he stayed for a good while before removing his shoes. Then he felt ready to explain the ways in which he was bereft. He staggered into the hall. His neighbor wouldn't let him use her phone. Fine, fine, fine. It almost was. He might have said "bereft," but to whom? And how? He could not remember the pregnant woman's number, much less her name.

Put That Thang in It Face

THE SUBJECT HAD NO IDEA THAT CARPENTER ANTS were marching across his porch, around the glider and plants, to a moth's corpse. He did know that the air was fresh and the light was true, so he took his boy out there to play with trucks. He used them to illustrate rhyming words: "crash," "smash," "bash."

The boy played and smiled, but he did not speak. The Subject wondered if the boy loved the Subject's wife more than him. He ached over this likelihood, but he understood the boy's preference, for his wife had breasts, and the tenderness they implied was real.

Under their bed, she kept a special box which held a variety of thrilling toys. The box was adorned with painted men and women of every race, all naked and fruitfully engaged. These figures were set in relief and, in certain private moments, the Subject liked to run his hands over both the men and the women. The box was secured by two metal snaps like those found on lunchboxes of the last century. It had a lunchbox's handle too, which neither the Subject nor his wife deigned to use.

The boy played with his trucks. The Subject daydreamed of the box. Neither of them noticed the harvesting ants. The next morning, though, the Subject found the body of a white bug in the boy's closet. It suggested a race of bugs growing in the walls. When his wife called it a booger, he screamed. Halfway down the stairs, though, he began to suspect that it was indeed a booger.

Their new home, deep in the city's urban core, had numerous problems: clogged pipes, mold damage, and holes forming in the shapes of celebrity silhouettes. The holes were often no larger than toddler fists. The Subject had no experience with any tool more serious than a hammer, so, soon after moving in, he began asking his neighbor Dave for help. The Subject paid him in beer. Dave felt the six-pack for coldness, then taught him how to fill the holes with plaster and sand the patchwork clean. The Subject felt more upright after he had scrubbed and smoothed away the profiled heads of Kanye West (second floor, hallway), Taylor Swift (boy's room, above the bay window), Meryl Streep (master bathroom, northeast of the toilet), and Oprah Winfrey (master bedroom, wall behind the door).

On another occasion, Dave rejected the Subject's proposed light switch. "You put that switch on that circuit, you gone have fire." Dave hunted his tool chest for a 20A. Then he showed the Subject how to strip wire and make the proper connections. "Pay heed. Match wire to screw or you house gone burn."

"I would not want to have a fire," the Subject said.

"Heh. You talk funny, Android."

That night, the Subject put down his book and asked his wife whether or not he looked funny. He said he had felt each of his cheeks in turn and that they seemed to be made of rigid plastic. Also, several expressions hurt him to employ, as when he had earlier disciplined the boy in part with a look he called "stern." His wife said he did not look funny to her. He gave her the stern look. She laughed. She bade him relax and pulled out the box. She put the ball in his mouth and tied the gag. For a time, he did not worry about his cheeks.

At Dave's yard sale, people crowded around tables of t-shirts, ceramic pots, detective novels, and miscellany. They shared a fine spending mood. Dave made the rounds, squatting to joke with every child, opining on drought and traffic patterns with every adult. Dave's wife collected money in a tin bucket. The neighbors, hauling away their new junk, admired his love for people.

The Subject helped him fold up chairs at the sale's end. They worked till a passing pick-up shoved rap music through their bodies. The driver circled the block to punish them a second time. The kid in the truck's bed took a picture of them with a phone. The Subject wondered what the kid might do with such a picture. Could the kid write a caption? If asked, would he understand what the Subject meant by the word "caption"?

Dave asked, "Ain't them boys sad through and through?"

The Subject wanted to say something about the humble origins of Abraham Lincoln and how one could not predict the man for the boy. Instead, he studied the impression a chair's round foot had left in the dirt. It was somehow square. He watched that ground for two minutes.

"Hey, Android," Dave said, knocking his own skull. "You okay in there?"

The Subject had never seen a man knock his own skull to underline that question. He pointed to the square as though it might be an answer, but the square was round.

The following weekend the Subject's wife took the boy to visit her parents south of town. The Subject had begged off the trip, saying that the careful analysis of certain files he'd brought home might earn him lunch with upper management. But, alone, the Subject put aside that work in favor of jazz and masturbation. He found, in the boy's room, a storm of white bugs. They made him their tornado's eye. They dotted the bed, dresser, toy chest, and collection of stuffed bears. He rescued the trucks.

Soon, Dave pointed his flashlight under the bed and along the walls. He could not find even the crack through which they had come. "You sure you saw bugs?" he said. "I know maggots is white. Don't know no white bugs. Maggots leave slime. You know that?"

The Subject wrote: *Now there is one property that bugs must have in common with plants. For some plants are generated from the seed of plants, whilst other plants are self-generated through the formation of some elemental principle similar to seed: and of these latter plants some derive their nutriment from the ground, whilst others grow inside other plants, as is mentioned, by the way, in ancient Greek literature on Botany. So with bugs: some spring from parent bugs according to their kind, whilst others grow spontaneously and not from kindred stock; and of these instances of spontaneous generation some come from putrefying earth or vegetable matter or walls of homes, whilst others are spontaneously generated inside of neighbors, from the secretions of their several organs.*

He had not believed in spontaneous generation till the words came from his pen. He folded the paper into a thick rectangle and kept it in his pocket.

Dave entered the Subject's backyard and shot a raccoon savaging an open bag of trash. The bullet went through its temple. The Subject came outside, put a thumb to his cheek, and moved the skin and underlying plastic in a circle. Raccoon material settled like jelly on his lawn and his garbage. Skull parts were scattered about and were indistinguishable from rocks. He could have hosed the blood for many hours but, he knew, some of it had already bonded forever to the soil. Dave made a stop sign of his palm. "You best sit," he said. "This beyond your program."

The Subject leaned against his back door. He studied a point above and beyond Dave's head, a point marking nothing particular. Not the shadowed treeline. Not the fence in need of leveling. Not the haunted-seeming REO home with shredded paint and rotten boards that he had once showed the boy in a hollow threat. His eyes functioned as usual, but his brain did not receive their transmissions. A light grew inside the point, a light made of something worse than sunset.

The boy clutched the Subject's jeans. The Subject could not remember the names of the couple who stood on their patio and lifted their wine in praise. Two boys ran up the driveway. Dave let them see and smell the body. The taller one said, "He put that thang in it face!" The shorter one took its picture with his phone. They saluted Dave, and Dave saluted them, all with the seriousness of military officers at a hero's funeral. The boys sprinted off, laughing.

Dave bagged the kill. He asked, "You want know why I call you 'Android'?"

The Subject did not.

In bed, he imagined white bugs eating their way out of Dave's head, revealing a brain tattooed with Hebraic script that was the Subject's new name.

His wife donned a new corset that reminded them both of life before the boy. She tied him to the bed and said she missed that easy time. She gagged him when he tried to apologize. He moaned when she tied him hard to the bedposts. His wrists burned open. She made love to him. He kept bone still when white bugs crawled from her hole.

He brought the boy outside to test a new remote-controlled dump truck. Its carriage rose and fell with the touch of a button, tumbling rocks and action figures down the porch steps. It had great power drive, and the Subject used it to crash the old trucks into the railing. "Vroom! Vroom!" the Subject said. The boy gathered the victims and rolled them around. The Subject took the boy's shoulder. The boy turned. White bugs marched from his eyes.

The Subject was reduced to hoping that, one day soon, in the downstairs bathroom, above the toilet roll dispenser, a hole shaped like his wife's head would appear. She would not see the resemblance, but he would, and so would the boy. The Subject and his son would insist on their view many times over the course of two or three days, the Subject waving rulers and protractors and tacking beside it profile shots of her in her mid-twenties, the boy dragging her to the hole and calling it "Mama." The word would fly through him. It would give him wings.

In bed again, the Subject did not share any of those visions with his wife, but tried to explain in safer terms that he worried about himself as a father. She rolled over.

"The box?" he said.

He led the boy to the master bedroom, opened the snaps, and let the boy dump its contents onto the carpet. For a long while, the boy was happy to put the toys in the box and dump them out again. Then he began to play rough, but the straps and buckles made it hard for him to throw the ball-gag with any success.

"What do you have?" the Subject asked before every toss.

The boy pulled the wraps belt-like around his waist.

"What are those?" the Subject asked.

The boy tested each vibrator as though one might be a magic wand or drumstick.

"What is it? What is it?"

A bug the size and color of a hundred-watt bulb grew from the light fixture. The Subject felt sure it was the queen. The boy hugged his leg so it could not bend. The queen flew down in a slow spiral, yet the Subject failed to swat it dead. He kicked the boy off him, took up the ball-gag, swung and failed again. The queen landed on his forehead. She had no eyes, no face. A thin white proboscis grew from her blank head. She ran it through his nose. Light charged through him.

The boy yelled, "Da! Buh!"

The Subject yelled other words. They all sounded wrong to him.

My Assets

I

Hey

Often sounds leered. A probe. Sometimes gentle, sometimes not. Retains little to no resale value.

Body

A dream, I've heard.

Venusian. Singular.

Bangin, bumpin, good good lovin.

Intact. Used.

Mine, I've heard. Theories of ownership vary from state to state, nation to nation, culture to culture.

Milk

Cow product.

Prevents cancer. Good. One disease already put me to bed.

Roommates A and B want some. They get none. They don't get names either. No one should. They say naming names helps what understand whom, but how would they know?

Ideas

Bodies fatten and die. Ideas last, Daddy says.

Checking account

Current balance: $376.11. Even after _____, I remain a budget queen.

II

Condoms

Roommate A says they negate feeling, which is a problem for her, for some reason.

Ideas

Imagine some android programmed with a safe-sex imperative plus human need. I'd gouge the price of condoms if it came moaning around me.

Principles of Finance

Econ 101 textbook. Bought for $66.32. I saved the receipt in a hanging file as directed by Daddy, who preaches the regular recording of transactions. Daddy does not trust memory. Neither do I. Zero value in it. So I record. Learn what's mine.

Describes effect of scarcity on price.

Defines pure capitalism and its mongrel variants.

Textbook purchase price does not suggest resale value. College bookstores pay shekels on dollars for mint condition trade-ins, so I have scribbled and smeared ink all over its theories of ownership.

Daddy

Says ideas reflect values.

Says, "Play dumb, okay, when strangers approach. That'll keep you safe."

Fallible.

Mommy

Who?

III

Roommates A and B

Returns diminish with use.

Study from afar the progress of my disease. Watch *Dr. Oz*. Turn up the volume so I must endure his quack sales pitch. They do it every day, as though programmed.

You get what you pay for or you're worth what you're paid. So I might sell them to Turks on the internet. Maybe Russians. The Eastern Option is theoretical, makes me feel a pencil scratching in my head, but a businesswoman can never dismiss potential profits.

Breasts

Have earned positive male reviews in rooms both well-lit and not. Ladies give praise and daggers. A transgender boy called them best in show. They are beloved, I think.

Light brown areolas and nipples.

Pert. Bra not always strictly necessary.

I might earn six figures for them if I could swap parts like an android, but I cannot. Breasts only work as part of a complete body, which includes, alas, narrow subjectivity and thirst for milk.

Ideas

You're worth what's been paid. Lightbulbs and skinny jeans are, therefore, good ideas. Their makers' progeny can eat babies dipped in liquid gold, if they want. The acquisition of capital has liberally expanded their range of dining options.

IV

Milk

Better than meat. No need to butcher a cow. Just set a bucket and tug its udders. Spare its life. It might be sore in the afternoon, but it lives, mostly.

Make-up kit

Includes all you dream. Will make you look hot and brainless. I recommend brainless. You see where brains end.

Milk

An all-dairy diet can light hell in digestive and excretory systems. That doesn't sound like an asset, but trust me. I've nursed this gallon since dawn. Wrecked the programs of Roommates A and B. After one emission, they got sour-mouth faces as though they had sucked lemons from a sewer. Roommate A donned her gas mask. She and her friends usually wear it when inhaling/exhaling weed for double or triple-effects. She's a fat, dream-headed stoner, but today's mask is about me.

They haven't asked me to come in the living room and watch *Dr. Oz*.

You see the value?

You're welcome, cows.

V

Bed

One half of Daddy's move-out gift. Oak frame and headboard. Stained. Mattress used for known purposes. Hidey space underneath. Dark so I can see out, no one in.

Bureau

Gift's other half. Rises to the average female's nose level. Stores panties, running clothes, socks, condoms, dust, germs, whatever's been forgotten, which is best.

Cows

Can't remember their milkings. Happy.

Roommate B

Doesn't buy milk diet idea.
Talks. Hops. Scrubs kitchen.
Cow-killer.
Android. I know. Her machine eye glows, subtle but true.

Ideas

Humans are androids pretending to help, wrecking assets.
See man coming? Turn cow.
Dumb cow, happy cow.
Moo.

VI

Hair

Since puberty's onset, on all dates save _____, this hair has been treated according to the rinse-repeat method espoused by esteemed stylists throughout the western world, using the highest quality, most expensive products on the market.

Has been called silky and luscious. Has been combed, sniffed, licked, pulled, and chewed by male partners. Therefore valuable. Roommate B dreams this hair. She's told me so in golder days. She wants it even when she pities me. That pity/want combo means another value downgrade for Roommate B.

Eyes

Oriental, I've heard, though I am moon white.

Switch color at every solstice and equinox and also with temperature drops and rises of three-plus degrees, but, in general, the switches are random from green to baby to dark blue. Cannot recall color on ____. Good.

Legs

Model quality, I've heard. Attractive legs are said to increase a woman's marital prospects to young men of ambition and promise, or to older gents whose ambition and promise has been fulfilled and who are now ready to drown their wives and children in exchange for three wet thrusts.

Toes

Have that often sought and rarely found perfect symmetry.

Lips

Pink. Full. Moist. Like to sell them off and quit words. But every android would see and ask, with programmed pity, "What happened?"

Shadow

More loyal than dog. Less cleanup than cat. Useless in fight. Quiet, at least.

VII

Principles of Finance

This is pure capitalism: at the meat market, which is Android City, which is everywhere, you are desired, caressed, scooped, groped, massaged, fingered, thumbed, pinched, gripped, and so on. Your value is being appraised.

T. Salzburg

_____.

~~*Names*~~

Principles of Finance

Relationships are composed of material exchanges based on mutually determined appraisals of value. They cannot involve dreams. They should be drowned, like wives and children, in a neighbor's pool.

Wardrobe

I've got anything you want to look brainless in, except clothes from ____. Those are gone, unless you find that dumpster at that gas station whose name I've forgotten, which is good, west or south of here. You'll never find them, and there'd be no point. Points and clothes are for androids seeking androids, not me. Forget that. Go cow. Eat grass. Behave.

VIII

Sense of Proportion

No one event outweighs the sum total of your experiences. Life goes on, as songs fellate.

Appears functional in public, though Roommate B says it is not the be-all-end-all and neither is beauty, but what does she know? She's never owned either, nor has she bought milk on any wrong night. She clicks, whirs, drips fluid. I?

Ideas

Android City has an economy based on take rather than exchange. Androids milk you for sustenance. You cope. It could be worse. It is. Androids are human. You are android. Not cow. Your programming has been wrecked. Have milk. Be relieved. You're no cannibal.

Daddy

Calls me Pumpkin, Smurfette, Isabelle, Muffin, Sweetheart, and Turnip. Don't ask. The story's between him and me. Not as strong as I once believed. Poor reader of body language and vocal tone. Benevolent. Puffy with dreams, though old, balding, gray. Irons pants and dabs cologne on his neck before grocery trips. A cheeriness. Votes in spite of political disappointment. Trusts cops and neighbors. Edgy about his new black neighbors. Goes out of his way to loan them tools. Encourages sorority membership, wants more, says to get involved, to put it all on the resume. If he knew, he'd want to kill. Good man. Thinks me good. Wrecks idea of me as either android or cow.

Milk

Last drops. Most stores are closed. At the gas station, T. Salzburg leers. "Hey." So many heys. Returns diminish with use. Not this one.

____.

Play dumb, as advised. Cope as android or cow. Fail. Too many assets remind us. We remain sick, human.

Do the Fish

Describe your first understanding of manhood.

We must have confused the hill of junk in the pick-up's cab with a touch of glory. Then Dad put the truck in reverse and flattened a German shepherd. He said the dog must have wanted this end, because more head than body opened onto the tire path. Clumps of fur and bone were carried downslope by varicolored ooze. I fetched Dad's gloves. They were suede and triple-stitched, meant for gripping lumber and sheetrock. Dad said to put the dog in the receptacle. We had not yet solved the maggot problem therein. I think I was the only one calling it a problem. The maggots slimed around and atop bags of rancid meat. Dad said to leave the gloves with the dog. He'd have to buy another pair. His tone conveyed my fault. Then it was off to the scrapyard, where he pocketed thirty-seven dollars, tax-free.

Connect the past to the present.

How that life could have spiraled into my daughter, I don't know. But my wife was gone, and Terri spent too much time in overalls. She, an eight-year old, once told me that she would "evolve into a dude." I briefly retired from the back porch. I returned with a whiskey sour and a pink note card from which I read platitudes on the topic of dads loving their girls as is. She wasn't having that lameness. She meant to be otherwise.

Define her in greater detail.

She had robot toys that are today called vintage. She did not collect them. She played with them. It was no use explaining to her that boys of the Reagan era generally agreed that Go-Bots were garbage knockoffs for the aesthetically dumb. She made me invest real dollars in Breez, who bent into a ceiling fan. As a robot, he had a single foot that might have been a phallus.

Say "Freedom."

Easy enough.

Do it.

Freedom. Happy?

Offer tangential details relevant to your dealings with Terri.

Soon after that conversation, I began to date a man who identified as a woman. Olivia was pre-op, and their original parts were still intact. But, under hormone therapy, they were beginning to grow breasts. Also, they were a habitual exfoliator. They applied creams to their legs, pits, and crotch. Our caressing, you can imagine, was a greasy affair.

Four years prior, they had quarterbacked their way to the Class-A state championship, which sounded like the third qualification I sought in a lover: a parental lead.

Illustrate the relationship between lover and daughter.

You'd think Olivia would have found Go-Bots campy in that gay way, but you couldn't talk to them about gay, and when Terri showed off Cy-Kill, they said what almost anybody conscious knew: "Those things suck."

Recall your daughter's response.

She said she wished these were biblical times.

Recall your response to her response.

None of us, not even her, wanted to hear that sentence's missing "because."

Surprise us.

If, given the dog anecdote and the tension between Terri and Olivia, I told you that my lover was enamored of tropical fish, and that they had moved their aquarium into our living room and made it the centerpiece therein, set atop a coffee table on which my daughter played regularly, would you know where this story was headed, and would you be disappointed by that knowledge?

Justify your choice of bedmate.

The first qualification was that they could not make me a two-time father.

Advance time.

That autumn, we operated as well as we could in a situation meant to comfort me, if no one else, until the school summoned me in regard to my daughter's writing.

Detail your hopes.

Generic.

Detail, we said.

A father hopes that when he is called about his child's writing, he shall be commended. Perhaps a third party shall describe a contrast between his parenting and that of his departed dad. Perhaps he shall sit stoically during this description—or shall he instead bask in the glow of social affirmation? But he knows that his original hope, like all hopes, is sadder than any school system. Teachers have no time to praise.

Name the officials present.

Principal and Teacher. I cannot be more specific.

Gauge them, sexually.

Genetically ill-favored. Bag bodies, downturned mouths. Their forebears had driven ancient men to flagellant hate of their bodies.

Summarize the officials' attack.

They were willing to tolerate her tomboyishness a far stretch. They would accept the popular use of her nickname, "Truck," on the playground, but would not approve a written record of her gender-bending ambition. The students would share their work, and she would be mocked by her peers. In short, a girl could not say that, when she grew up, she wanted to be a father.

Defend her.

I did not say this to either official present, but grammar and punctuation posed Terri no challenge. The subjects, verbs, and objects in that paragraph had been well-chosen. Her prepositions, long her bane, were appropriate. Every word had been arranged for maximal effect: every sentence ended with a ka-pow.

Outline your actual response to their attack.

1. Studied my right thumb's lengthy nail.

2. Determined to clip the nail before bed.

3. Made real and imaginary words by rearranging the letters of "yellow."

Include your lover in this scene.

It could not have ended otherwise. Wherever they went, people were drawn to them. In that way, they reminded me of dead old Dad, who said that "people hardly matter, especially you, which is why you need me to tell you how to go." Olivia's white skirt rode high up their thighs. They crossed and uncrossed and recrossed their legs in the same Sharon Stone homage they had used on me that summer. It had, I knew, a brain-sloshing effect.

Take as much time and space as needed to finish the scene.

Principal said this could not work.

"What 'this'?" Olivia said.

"This. This." She waved generally.

We stood. Teacher's eyes were directed past us, toward crown molding above the door.

"That?" Olivia said. "That works. It's the best part of the room."

"No," Principal said.

"What then?"

"This." Her hand fell, though she meant to point it at them. Words like "stability" and "maternal figure" dribbled from her, but they lacked predication. We stood in a square around a desk overrun with ballpoint pens and memos. The heap was topped by the paragraph detailing Terri's dream. It seemed that a moral of tolerance was about to be unwound, but Olivia took up their purse. They flashed their teeth. Those teeth were model-quality white. They were justly proud.

Confess.

It is true that almost anybody conscious knows that Go-Bots suck. I roomed outside that "almost." Some mornings, Terri would wake to find her Cy-Kill other than where she had left it. I would joke about poltergeist, but I had been nostalgic again.

Confess more.

Dad shared none of his scrap money with me, so I had to shoplift for toys. Cool boy Transformers were too large, boxed, and well-guarded, but Go-Bots practically begged to be stolen in their easily ripped open packaging. I must have been caught on camera dozens of times, like when I swiped Cop-Tur from the drug store. His blades made my pocket look home to four pitiful erections. Management gave me a wide berth.

Contrast the two brands of toy.

While a Transformer required ten to fifteen moves to bend a race car into a comedian with guns, even my favorite Go-Bot, the aforementioned Cy-Kill, took five total. Moreover, Go-Bots had neither elbows nor knees. They were moronically designed so, for instance, one of Jeeper-Creeper's wheels became his ear—a single ear with no corresponding wheel-ear on its head's other side. Fortunately, they had the Last Engineer.

Say what is in your hand.

Samples of Olivia's hair. Facial, I believe.

Continue the contrast.

Okay. I'm talking about the story behind the toys and what makes it work. In the midst of a civil war, the Last Engineer developed the technology to transfer his dying world's heroes into mechanical bodies, thereby ensuring the survival of their best men. But the bad guys got hold of new bodies too, so the conflict was upgraded. If you're thinking that the writers of the Go-Bots imagined the singularity, well, no, but in the finest sci-fi tradition they rigged the future of science to their subliterary purpose. Anyhow, the Go-Bots sought this Last Engineer who, they presumed, could restore them to their lost flesh, complete with bending limbs.

Tell us how you rigged their story to fit your purpose.

What I wanted, what every Go-Bot quest I played out in the kitchen before Dad came home and asked me what the hell I was doing at fourteen with those dork toys that he thought he'd gotten rid of with the dog—not that dog but my dog—was for the Last Engineer to extract the last bit of consciousness from us both, because brains and hearts were exhausting superfluities. We'd be left a pair of family machines.

Tell us about freedom.

Couldn't I further describe a well-refined though peculiar teenage nihilism?

Tell us.

You put a corpse or love in its appointed receptacle and declare it stored. You cover it. Later, you look inside, discover even the maggots have gone.

Surprise us with an item in your closet.

Given abundant time in an empty house, I have stitched together a compellingly accurate Cy-Kill costume. Every color and detail is correct, down to the voided yellow eyes. Its wearer can bend his arms and knees. That wearer cannot, however, become a thick-wheeled chopper.

Elaborate on the emptiness of your house.

The house still contains what houses must contain to support modern life: dishwasher, nukable meals, and porn sorted by fetish. On the other hand, it is newly lacking in Go-Bots and Sharon Stone skirts. It will never lack shed hair.

Explain what led to that emptiness.

I brought my daughter outside and, before all those bugs and trees, recounted my lover's heroism vis-a-vis school. She nodded. She said that "heroism" might be too strong a word, though she admitted that Olivia had acted in her defense. She could respect that. A thing was missing from Terri's assessment. I knew that much.

Set the hair beside the aquarium.

Okay.

Go to your room.

Okay.

Put on the costume.

Okay.

Resume your position on the couch.

Okay.

Continue the explanation.

Okay. Neither of them was interested in legalized rearrangements, and I hadn't the character for pursuit. They left a single note, with Olivia's name scratched beneath Terri's cursive. It was a scramble of platitudes which described a feeling of love for me, or rather a "Love, but" feeling which I knew well. In my life, I have not always been lonely, not even often lonely, because no one will leave alone anyone willing to be led. I had learned that with many loves came many buts.

Recall your lover's feeling for the aquarium.

Their feeling was not so much for the container as for the fish inside, especially the zebra fish, with stripes that looked painted on, and whose stupidity could not be metaphored. It sometimes ate the phony shells lining the bottom. They would study it for hours on end, with a face open to dreams.

Explain why a fish so beloved might be abandoned.

Is it not clear? Every love is pregnant with a but. The child was born.

Describe the appeal of Cy-Kill.

He does not feel.

Recall the second qualification.

I cannot.

Define your daughter in greater detail.

She was no rock of kid you composed by the writing of sentences, but whatever crawled beyond the words in your throat. Of course, she spit words like "evolve," and knew what they meant, almost, so you couldn't fool her for too long, though I had hoped otherwise.

Connect the past and present.

Your command brings to mind the old problem of cause and effect. You want to piece together who trashed which dog, while your daughter has taken a pre-op for a mom, herself for a boy, and a word for a dad, or as though the "who" and the "which" have a clear, one-way relationship, when they're really running their trucks over each other as a bit part of a fifty-car pile-up, and taking great pains at their work.

Describe an understanding of manhood.

It requires a fish brought into open air. It requires the fish to do its floppy best to convey its oncoming doom, and it requires that communication to go ignored. It requires a receptacle of any size, so long as it has a bottom. It does not require watching the fish die on a bed of thrown-out pasta, though that is acceptable. It requires the wearing of any costume to fail. A Cy-Kill costume, for instance, gives the appearance of voided eyes, but before the fish quits flopping, you will see too much.

---.

Tell me what to do next.

A Good Dog Would Forget

(1) **Make light!** See our father's chalky hair, baby ears, fogged eyes, the melting look of him—every bit a lie. Your fathers too, despite their casings, despite their presences, have gone. A good dog would forget what is dead. Then she would chew a suspicious toy, a father would bury her, and it would be his turn to forget a crime. We would build—are building—a room in which he can be remade.

(2) A serial number has been sewn to his neck. It may be a line of toppled urns or letters—we cannot tell for sure. No matter how we fasten, clip, and bind our father to the room, we cannot know him. We can say that his head smells of burnt butter, but what part of him does not? His hands, Yes, but we feel unready to talk of hands. Instead, we put a scalpel flat to his left cheek. We take heart from sitcom endings. We appreciate the contrast between deep space and the puddle of soda beneath the lamp.

(3) We cut a square around the serial number. No blood leaks. We peel back the skin, remove the bone and wire, and find the steel box of memory. Our father's box made sea from land. He listened to us recount a twenty-year past Seder and said, No, the afikomen was taped under the table or, No, the dog went crazy before you moved out, and it crapped the living room, not your bed, or, No, your first car was a Mitsubishi, and we paid half for it, so quit whining or, No, the hair on your plate was too mossy to have been mine or, No, the secret room was meant to store tools, not maps.

(4) If you deny knowing, much less building, any secret room, the father may smoke from the eyelids. From the open head, a sound may come which recalls a lightbulb being crushed underfoot. We do not know what you would do next, but we would extract the box from its

housing. We would set it beside the fresh jug of soda. The bluff might work, as we would be far from the reunion party. The walls would be full of modern spray-foam insulation. We would declare ourselves made of foam. We would ask if he understands what that implies. If he smokes on, we would rewire the box and hope for the best. We would install a bay window and count the amorphous swallowing stars.

(5) The reshaping gifts of machines—these may be distinguished and classified. A dog, for instance, tears open throw pillows and every kind of sock. A car seat mangles posture. A fence line mucks our view of the neighbor girls when they kneel in its shade, even when we watch from the balcony. A needle ends a dog, and one corner of fence thereafter marks her home. Our father often reshaped with a single No, but he once ordered us to plant fruit trees all about the yard. His goal appeared to be a new polygamy, a ripe marriage of us to dirt and pomegranates. Our father wanted at least one hard-skinned fruit in the family. He wanted to end our homebodies. He wanted a lake out back, too, eventually, with every class of fish and with all that eat them. He wanted grandchildren. Multiply, he said.

(6) Our memory is less box than Temari ball. Its design—improvised pricks and drags of the needle. Its colors—a range of gray. Its threads—we must delay this topic until we have done with the hands. Ready? No. From the study of mortuary practices, we can learn the various reshaping gifts of men. The Egyptians, of course, embalmed their dead. Pagans taught Catholics to cremate the fallen. Jews must bury their losses. Outside Manila, Caviteño tribesmen carve out trees and die in the hollowed trunks. Mongolian transmigrationists cut their dead loves into strips of meat, haul them up a mountain, and feed them to vultures. When those vultures fly into the sun, their meals are given new bodies. In every land, among every people, a beloved pet is treated like family. It is consequently subject to the local practices of men, though not always. Fish are either flushed or eaten. A father has never fit into a toilet. He, too, is subtracted according to custom, but he also remains locked in a secret room. We make and remake him day and night. We do not hope for rest.

The Blattarian Model

After his wife and son went to meet the eye specialist, the father knelt midway up the stairs and cut at the banister's thirteenth rib. He used the hacksaw that the house had compelled him to buy at Kornin's Fine Tools. Its titanium blade proved worth the expense. The surrounding stairs, along with his jeans and wrists and hands, were soon whitened by sawdust, and the rib came free. Blue and green wires spewed from its ends. He pulled from inside the rib a circuit encased in black plastic. Its flashers faded out in his palm. He noted more severed wires at the banister's base. He understood immediately that they pumped electric blood all through the house.

A roach crawled onto his shoe. It rested at the lip and stared him down. It was likely an agent of the house. One roach meant three hundred more were breeding in the walls. The father had to be patient. He wanted to see what its friends would do.

He had believed for weeks that the house made his mind happen, that his memory, among other assets which everybody called human, was the product of a binary or perhaps trinary code. His throat caught, though, whenever he considered his belief's first corollary: that his family existed within the confines of the house and nowhere else. He choked on the second corollary: that his family existed only when he saw them. But the more tools he bought, the easier he breathed.

One day, he was entering data at the office when a related disorienting idea occurred to him: the house contained his world. The office appeared to be located on the fourth floor of a glassy suburban plaza, but it actually occupied the same space as the family's dining room. When he got high in the parking lot with Matt and Tom, he was also in the garage. He was there, too, when he shopped at Kornin's. The eye specialist's office was located in a half-bathroom which the house compelled him to avoid. He had not yet determined the location of the zoo, where he, his wife, and his son had recently enjoyed a great many habitats and captives. He often tried to map the rooms to which supposedly different destinations belonged, or to chart out the hundreds of places that could be found in his foyer alone, but he lost the maps almost as soon as he drew them, his charts became illegible with his overlapping notes and designs, and then his boss would call him into a meeting.

The flashers appeared superfluous, but he knew that by their lights the house compelled him up and down the stairs, to purchase hack-saws and bistouries meant for dolls more than men. The house's intentions were obscure but, he hoped, not malicious. It often compelled him to remember a phone left downstairs before he completed his ascent. Then again, if the house meant only to help him, it would have compelled him to remember the phone before he went up.

His wife and son appeared to enter through the front door. They were coated and gloved, his wife's hand on his son's head, his son's hand on her purse's zipper. She called the father downstairs without acknowledging the banister's wreck.

His son doted, as usual, on the stuffed, pink giraffe. Since the zoo trip, that toy had not been far out of his reach. The boy had an expectable amount and arrangement of limbs, hair, and mouth, plus one fully-functioning eye, but the father saw and remembered these features only as the hazed background of the bad eye, which he viewed in sharp focus. Its pupil did not rest in the eye's center. A rogue muscle pulled it toward the nose. The boy's condition had been named several times in the father's presence but, despite his focus, the father had never been able to name it when asked to do so, nor could he name it now. The boy was supposed to wear a patch over the good eye to strengthen the bad one, but he would not wear the patch unless and until he wanted to play pirate. The boy played pirate on occasion, but not as often as he or his wife would have liked.

The couple soon sat opposite each other at the table while his son crashed the hardwood floor with his toy. In the boy's hands, the giraffe became a truck with loud brakes and a louder horn. Then it became a saxophone. His son blew into the giraffe's head and made buttons of its neck spots. The father did his best to ignore this foolery. His wife, meanwhile, discussed the muscle. She named it. In Latin. Though the father immediately forgot the word, she prided herself on this lingual knowledge. Her green eyes had darkened in the months following their son's birth, then lightened, then darkened again whenever talk turned to the boy's condition. She kept her graying black hair tied in a ponytail nearly all the time the father observed her. The father wished the house would compel his wife to lower her hair more often, and not in the dark, and not merely as a preface to its washing. Her face, though, offered no reason for complaint. It remained soft-boned and young no matter time, setting, or hairstyle. Its constancy involved the regular application of creams. It was the fond envy of her lady friends. While she described the operation, he held the circuit in his lap. He touched its dead lights. She said the specialist and his team would drug their son, peel back the lid, aim a laser, and snip the muscle. The pupil would return forever to its normative position, and the boy would be able to partake of life and love as he wished, with either man or woman, because their acceptance of him and his future life was virtually certain if not formally agreed upon.

He heard his wife speak through the medium of the house.

What, she had asked the doctor, were the dangers of a misaimed laser? The bastard had chuckled. He was the best they could afford to go into debt with, but he did not respect her. She wished for the umpteen-thousandth time that the father had accompanied them, if only to prevent such condescension. The father set his hands on the table, palms up. The house did not compel him to speak. She went on. The doctor said that a misaimed laser could lead to a permanent sensitivity to light or, worse, a permanent insensitivity to light.

"Blind," she said. "Blind."

The doctor said not to worry. The chances were miniscule. A misaimed laser would land him on the evening news, and he did not intend to land, ever, on the evening news.

The father touched the circuit. He studied the ponytail. The hair fell from the tie in a junk of curls. Yet his look must have appeared tender. Perhaps a sense of their shared burden came through it. Perhaps it reflected her anxieties related to the eye specifically and to parenthood generally. She asked him for his hands, and he gave them, and she set hers upon them, and they seemed to agree.

He did not know what they had agreed upon.

He did know that the house had compelled his look and her response. He thanked the house for its help.

He wore a miner's cap for light. The otherwise dark garage smelled of potting soil, mulch, and stale smoke. Lawn tools and bikes hung from hooks in the ceiling. Dishes and knick-knacks from before the marriage were stacked in boxes. Standard hand tools were stored and labeled in a wide, locked chest. Specialty tools were kept in a smaller but better loved chest. The washer and dryer thrashed at laundry. Floridian pseudo-winter snuck under the doors. In the room's center, he took the stool at his workbench and smoked a joint down to a roach. He sipped water. Then he opened his bag of knives and selected the shortest, finest blade among them, the .5, not the only blade in the set which his wife called useless, but one of them, certainly. He wedged it into the border between the circuit-casing's front and back. After he popped it open to the metal guts, he removed his cap and aimed his penlight. As he expected, the wafers and pins had been arranged in a kind of blueprint of the house. Every circuit, he surmised, was partly a map.

The kitchen-shaped wafer contained a switch the size of one stubble of hair, but it was solid enough. He applied his tweezers, and the wafers lit up, and the wires snapped at him. When he flinched, the circuit latched onto his workbench. The newly powered bench rattled toward him. He hammered it dead. Then he found a roach mucking about the wreck's border.

He caught it in a jelly jar meant for the storage of screws. The roach scampered round and pressed its feet and antennae to the glass. The father set the jar beside the circuit. He grabbed a long pin, unsealed the cap, and stuck the roach through the back. The roach smoked and sparked. The smoke tasted like weed. He did not mind the waste of a specimen. The house, he knew, would send more.

Most nights, he wandered from room to room, though he always ended by his son's bed. The boy honked and snorted through a kind of whiffled congestion. The house put the sound into his son and the word "whiffled" into the father's head, compelling him to think of the white plastic ball he had supposedly hammered around yards as a child, though the metaphorical ball here was gobbed with snot. Down the hall, his wife snored a louder, feminine double of his son's bad breathing. His son slept, uncovered, on his back, in plaid pajamas, one hand shielding his heart, the other clutching the giraffe in a gentle half-nelson. His eyes fluttered with dreams.

The father set down both toolbox and circuit and pulled up a rocking chair. Along the floor's molding, roaches trooped from shadow to light to shadow. He wondered what tool would serve the purpose. The house ought to have told him but did not. The boy's bad eye cracked open. It glowed with fractional intelligence. The father would share that assessment with no one, though he thought it more honest than harsh, less personal than a problem endemic to the boy's age, for the brain of a two-year old Einstein could not have impressed him, much less the brain of his son. The boy battered walls with giraffes and wet his pants every second hour. The father's thoughts were presently interrupted by the noisy trickle of urine into his son's diaper. It spelled out the name of his son's condition: strabismus. Now, what a man might do with a word had long puzzled him, particularly words that were not English words. All words, foreign and domestic, he accepted on faith. Words, doctors, loves: these were religious articles. He set the circuit like a yardstick beside his son. He measured.

His wife lay in bed, lit moon blue by an infomercial. When he entered, she clicked on her lamp. He wanted to touch her cheek, but her hair was tied up, and a sheet of paper had been set on his pillow. She did not greet him. He stared into the open bathroom behind her. The shower curtain was drawn back to expose body washes and tile.

She read from the paper old critiques of him that he knew were printed in Castellar font. She did not mean to hurt him with the use of a foo-foo font, but the house surely did. He resisted the affront, as the house meant for him to resist, by tapping the circuit against his thigh. His wife paused to ask why he had been dragging that scrap around.

"Pondering," he said.

"Pondering."

"Wondering."

"Pondering, wondering what?"

"I don't know."

She folded the list and set it beside her lamp, which she clicked off, ending his view of the tile. TV light colored her legs. She had other words for him now. One of them was "love." She said this word with a heavy belt of faith. She said "doctors" too. "Understanding...Love... Doctors...Zoo." He came to the bed and unlaced his shoes. He stretched out beside her. The house sent him promises that he transmitted to her. She gripped and released his hand. She unmuted the TV. In a low but enthusiastic voice, a host swore that his machine produced the sweetest carrots of all time.

"Shall we call?" the father said.

His wife snored.

He held the circuit like a box of fragile bones. He could not see it well in that light, but that did not stop him from seeing.

In what room, he wondered, had they toured the zoo?

He had previously argued for the kitchen and, later, the dining room, prime sites of food and mange, but he settled that night upon the master bathroom. Excrement aside, both bathrooms and zoos pressed together real and artificial life. The African bush was fenced in. Dingoes slept in mud. Jaguars leapt behind glass. The father sat on the toilet. The house sent signals through the porcelain.

When had they gone?

Last week. His wife had organized a family day with sodas, photos, and fun in mind, but she forgot her camera at home. He smiled. His smartphone, he said, provided him with all but a butt wipe. She smiled. His son, leashed to a monkey-face backpack, smiled. They were together enough to enjoy a butt-wipe joke. Good.

Who held the lord's end of the leash?

Such questions were inessential, yet they compelled his attention. The father and his wife exchanged the duty every half-hour. The boy staggered in the lead, sometimes pulling the wife off-balance and sometimes pulling the cord so taut that he was jerked back. The father said his son was learning about equal and opposite reactions. Sunlight glared off head-shaped puddles. All around were families pretending they were alive, just as the father was pretending this memory was real. Space expanded and contracted, filled and emptied, according to the needs of the house. The people, animals, cages, and hot dogs fit inside a single shower tile.

Had they come only for the giraffe?

His son had, though the parents hoped to get their money's worth from the venture. They tried to hold off as long as they could, plying him with gifts and face-painting. The father asked if there wasn't some entomological exhibition around, but the boy, alone among boys, did not love bugs.

What did the foreign person call the giraffe?

The father did not understand the purpose of other languages. They seemed misfit in the house's scheme, like a hunk of meat caught in a back molar and hard to floss out. This foreign person, an Italian or French or Spanish androgyne, had paper skin and a voice that seemed damaged coming up the throat. They stood closely enough for the father to detect in them a hot lunch stink. They had a hunk of meat in their back molar. It was asteroidally shaped. They leaned into his son and called the animal by its foreign name. His son paid no attention to the oral disaster. The androgyne seemed invisible to all but one zoo-goer. Meanwhile, the father's wife had procured a branch of leaves for the boy to feed the giraffe. The androgyne whispered to the father a number of mispronounced and misused phrases in English. "Your purpose," the father said, "is to distract me. You are effective." The androgyne bowed. The son stuck his hand in the giraffe's mouth. Its teeth were large, cracked, buttery ice cubes. Its pink tongue reached out. His son extended the branch. His wife snapped pictures. His son faced him. In the giraffe's black mouth, the father saw ten thousand eyes.

A platoon of roaches made camp atop his new workbench. They crawled over their comrades' backs. They traced the perimeter. With their forelegs and antennae they bound the wires of the circuit to the bench's top. He squirted a straggler with Liquid Still, a chemical he had plucked from Kornin's bargain bin. He pinned the roach to a square of pegboard. His bistoury's hook was the size and shape of a steel infant's toenail, but he pushed it through the roach's skull without trouble and scooped out the eyes. He set them in a pudding dish. He smoked. Minutes, hours later, he put one eye under his microscope. Thousands of roach lenses came into view. The ommatidinal majesty quickened his blood. The single lens of his human eye was—by design—susceptible to objects of love, while this tiny roach eye viewed indifferently all but the red light of the world. The contrast proved to him the weakness of the human model.

The house had constructed their eyes.

If those eyes were improved, their minds would improve.

The house compelled him to know that.

He smoked. Roach eggs hatched. The new generation marched in a line up a wall, along the ceiling, down the rake, shovel, and family bikes. They did not interfere with him; he did not interfere with them. He foresaw a time when all his loose property would be appended to the house, each piece of it powered by a circuit, each circuit transmitting orders to him. He smoked. His hand-skin dried and split. The room ghosted at the edges. Night seemed to extend outward. Time, like space, could be balled up or unstrung at the house's command.

A roach crawled onto his shoe's lip, so he began. He filled the pudding dish with its and its brothers' eyes and left the sparking bodies where they dropped. Every so often he sifted through his harvest and crushed substandard eyes, trusting that he would gather enough suitable for his purpose. A third generation clogged the washer. He opened the dryer and a fourth generation emerged from the towels. Fragments of roach accrued on his fingers. He nibbled on dry granola. He cut and clipped and tied eyes together and failed. His wife entered on at least three occasions. She said impossible words like "Wednesday" and, the next time, "Thursday." The house must have compelled her to lie. He pulled out his soldering iron and burned to uselessness many fine eyes. Smashed parts and metal shavings tinted the concrete. His knuckles looked like bloody knots. His face hurt. His feet went numb. His elbows felt psoriatic. His mouth was too dry to speak aloud. A fifth and sixth generation wired both tool chests to the floor. They finished his granola. The garage smelled like a gaping wound. His wife came again with his son in tow. Her hair fell in mossy strings. His son must have lost his giraffe. The bad eye veered, as ever, noseward. His wife spat words the father knew to be English but which he could not follow. "Zoo?" "Androgyne?" He did not hear "Love." He quit paying attention when he learned how to proceed. Two eyes pressed together would, like happy rooms, latch onto each other. He smoked with gratitude, for this knowledge had been graced to him, not to the specialist. He would build a great compound of compound eyes. If every roach eye contained two thousand lenses, then a human-scale simulacrum might have two million lenses spying out the wide world. It would know them well.

His son said a name.

The father waved him off. I'm building you a gift, he thought he said. He raised the bistoury. When it is ready, I will call, and you will see.

The Remainder

Q: ARE YOU SURE THAT'S A CLOSET?
P: You don't trust me?
Q: Don't be hurt. It just looks—it does not look like a closet.
P: So? Open it. Find out.
Q: What's inside?
P: Three American daughters.
Q: Attractive?
P: Yeah. In different ways, of course. Sameness blows. You interested?
Q: Wait. Let's not wander off course too quickly.
P: Sure. Okay. But you know guys like us have never been hot properties. Someone's daughter might buy in for a minute, but she won't stick around, which hurts, yeah. After a few times, we drop out the market. We'd rather gorge on pizza and watch a ball game than deal with another American daughter. In a social manner, I mean. Too expensive on the heart.
Q: You said this? Or the neighbor?
P: Who?
Q: The neighbor. He's why I'm here.
P: Seriously?

Q: Summarize the neighbor's wheezing words.
P: All of them?
Q: Yes. Condense the complex whole into a sentence or three. Make it memorable.
P: Impossible. He went on and on. You know that, right?
Q: Were you the first to discover him?
P: Yeah. I think. This morning.
Q: Describe his physical position.
P: His limbs were in the right places, but twisted.
Q: Broken?
P: Not that I could tell. He had brownish wings of hair and a white flower in his mouth. His skin reminded me of skim milk. Not transparent, but that word midway between "solid" and "transparent." You know which one I mean. Had a milky scent too. I pinched the right cheek, made sure he was done. *(Pauses.)* That took more than three sentences. Okay?
Q: I am flexible.
P: Mmm. *(Pauses.)* Interesting.
Q: Please. Focus.
P: We could have fun.
Q: No. Never. Where was he, the neighbor, located?
P: On the laundry room floor.
Q: You said he was twisted?
P: In the shape of a gimmel.
Q: A what?
P: It's a Hebrew letter. I'll draw one. But—are you sure?
Q: Of?

P: You want to talk about him and not American daughters?
Q: That's a trick question.
P: Really?
Q: If I want to discuss your samples, I'm veering off track to prove my heterosexual bonafides. If I say otherwise, I seem less a man. No answer can make clear, simultaneously, my lust for daughters and commitment to the subject.
P: So you're tempted? Or not? Hey, the closet door is soundproof. Front door too. It's just you and me talking. Want to see what's inside?
Q: What's your game?
P: No game. I know your type. I'm your type. We're alike, you and I.
Q: How?
P: We're shy. Me, this morning I was tempted by an American daughter at Starbucks. Not a barista. Thin. Tall. So tall. Of all the dumb options, she read *Wuthering Heights*. She sounded out the words. Her lips moved. I almost approached her.
Q: Instead?
P: Went home. Today's laundry day.
Q: And?
P: Brought my load to the laundry room. Found the neighbor on the floor. Drunk, deceased, yeah, in the shape of a gimmel. He'd bought a packet of Tide from the dispensary, opened it, and went thump into that good night. The powder spilt. Detergent scent all in the air. That powder looked like a supersized rail of cocaine.

Q: Was the neighbor a drunk?
P: On numerous occasions, I called him Lush and Wethead. Not today, though. I'd never disrespect the dead with names. But I have evidence to back up the names, if you need it. Today, twisted, dead, he was still sweating vodka.
Q: Did alcohol hasten his end?
P: It happens. I've done it similarly, almost. Drunk till I napped. It comes so quick you can't worry about appearances. Yeah. Slept there till yeah.
Q: Do you think his drunkenness invalidates his words?
P: Nah. They're still words. English words. If you know English, you know them well enough, I think.

Q: Do we have faces?
P: Sure. We speak, don't we? We couldn't speak without mouths, which are exclusive to faces.
Q: Yes, but. Why such trouble?
P: I've read that the face serves as a lure in mate acquisition. The broad, forwardly directed nose—
Q: Do you believe that?
P: Yeah. Nah. The face may do plenty for other folks. Your face and mine, pal, have gotten us here.

Q: You're lying about the daughters.
P: Nah. At worst, they're hypothetical. The door, you can't disagree, is straight fact. Inspect it. I replaced the original closet door with a thicker model, one designed for a home's exterior. Sawed it off to fit the required dimensions.
Q: In violation of the lease?
P: Don't worry about that. Check out the rubber padding along the bottom. Seals the gap between door and floor. There's a micro-micro-millimeter's space anywhere along the door's sides and top. Beyond it, American daughters await. That's theoretical jabber to you, but I know. I built the sucker.
Q: Hm.
P: Let me show you the lock. I'm proud of the lock. Examine that beauty.
Q: It's fancy for a closet door. Again in violation of the lease.
P: I'll never apologize for a quality lock. The landlord should cheer for the upgrade.
Q: Would he?
P: The landlord's a landlord. That explains him, doesn't it? But the lock. It implies the value of what's inside. No key necessary. You enter the proper five-digit code and access a trove of earthly delights. When pressed, the buttons make soothing beeping sounds.
Q: That closet is neither wide enough nor deep enough to hold three American daughters.
P: That's how it looks, yeah. But they're tiny. "Petite" is the word, like we like them. Pliable. Secured, too, for men who can't afford heartbreak.

Q: Liar.
P: Prove me wrong.

P: Shapes define and limit. A summary is a shaping device. You draw lines around the essential. Cut, bend, tape, you know, to contain that essence within the shape's borders. What's outside, left over, the remainder, gets ignored.
Q: What are you doing?
P: Summarizing. That's what you wanted, right?
Q: Were those the neighbor's drunken, wheezed words?
P: I don't do transcripts. Not of any dead man's speech, anyhow. Dialect, wheezes, accents, timing, tone, none of that. Could seem disrespectful.
Q: But you have provided the gist?
P: Maybe. The value of any summary is conditional, yeah, upon the summarizer's memory, and memory is not the most reliable instrument.
Q: Say more about the remainder.
P: It can't know what the shape contains. It's outside. It can only theorize.
Q: It does not remember what came before the shape?
P: Exactly. It can believe, as you believe, that a closet is unlikely to contain American daughters. You need faith to believe otherwise, and faith must never be confused with knowledge. Obviously. Right?

P: Don't think too hard. I could enter the code. You could see inside real easy. Reach, touch, as you like.

Q: The neighbor. Your neighbor. That drunken, wheezing neighbor. Found in the laundry room. Contorted into a letter. Tell me.
P: What do you want to know?
Q: What he believed regarding shapes. A summary. Please.
P: His beliefs weren't clear. Been sorting them myself these past couple hours. He often considered the shape of death, yeah. What we know about it. Sounds pompous, right? Morbid, too, but who isn't morbid in these hard times?
Q: I do not deny morbidity of heart.
P: Hell, I pinched his cold right cheek.
Q: Will you summarize?
P: Okay. We stay outside the death-shape as long as we can, which is cool, but that position ensures that our knowledge of it will remain strictly theoretical. And how exactly is it shaped? How can it be measured? Analyzed? We can, at best, observe a few biological negations: end of blood flow, decay of flesh, absence of wife.
Q: Did the neighbor have a wife?
P: He had a woman. Or a man. A lover, yeah, who stayed for an extended period.
Q: Then what?
P: Left. That's the trouble.
Q: Then what?
P: Old story. The heart heals, but crooked. It wants new, different things, anything but family life.
Q: Then what?
P: A gimmel. For him, you, everybody. You know that, yeah. You've been around.

Q: I have. And you?
P: Sure. What do you think? That this morning's my first time clamming up around a tall American daughter? Man, that's why I built this closet. I'm not afraid to admit it. Not to you. We're the same. We're here together.
Q: Were you ever together with him?
P: In this very spot.
Q: Did you offer him the closet?
P: I did.
Q: Did he accept?
P: Who cares? He's dead. But you're here now. Front door's soundproof, like I said. It's you and me. In this closet are three American daughters. Secure, for men of our, yeah. Interested?

Sponsors

While his daughter was out on a date, Berg went to her apartment, slept with her roommate, and left with his head shaved to skin.

(Berg followed the program. He told me everything.)

When he returned home, he scrapped off segments of orange shampoo congealed to the shower walls. He wiped toilet paper at coiled hairs that had clung for months to the base of the tub. He rubbed his burning scalp.

His kitchen appliances were clean from disuse. He kept the pantry thinly stocked. A box of Raisin Bran, if granted life, could converse with the loaf of bread or box of Fudge Rounds on the shelf below it. Lonelier in the fridge was a package of salami. He had no strength for breakfast. He moved the new potholder (embroidered with a sunny-faced Jesus) from the stovetop to the trash can.

The tap water tasted like rotten egg smell. His daughter wanted him to bug the landlord for a filter, so disease couldn't come unbaited (*sic*, unabated) from the spout. Her English nettled him, but he would never correct her, because no one else worried about microbes eating him from the inside out. He hugged her whenever she had to drop an English course.

He carried an empty glass into the bedroom. He looked through its bottom and remembered the adjunct. They had been sleeping together for several weeks, but she had not seen his apartment. Similarly, his daughter's mother had never seen any place in which he had lived. He had slept with these and many other women, but he had slept with only two women in an apartment leased to him. His daughter's mother's father had inadvertently led him to the first of those women. Before Berg's daughter's Bat Mitzvah, he sent a letter threatening Berg with undesirable physical consequences if Berg, at the reception, did not keep to the ballroom corner farthest from the punch bowl. In that corner, he met someone willing to bring him punch and acknowledge his dignity. After he danced with his daughter, he brought this woman to his room. More recently, either last year or the year before it, he had gotten a flattop haircut that made him look military. At lunch, he stood taller than anyone else in the Burger King line. A bank teller coming in mistook him for someone else. He felt such rare magic that he bought her a chicken sandwich value meal, and she drove him home. He left too many people too poorly to worry over their names.

To make the bed, he kicked aside the sheet and leaned the mattress (a twin) Murphy-style against the wall.

His clean clothes were folded in a hamper set outside his closet. Whenever he felt ready to try sleep, he put his sobriety coin atop the clothes.

His room had impressed neither bank teller nor Bat Mitzvah guest. He understood. He preferred any woman's bedroom to his own.

He carried the glass into the living room. A six-string electric bass leaned against one corner. Berg had never played any instrument, though he had held this one in his lap a time or two and had felt the thickness of its strings. A friend had given him the bass, as well as an ivory chess set and a crystal vase, to hold. (I had given him no more than a sponsor's willing ear and advice.) He did not understand till much later that his friend was headed underground and that the goods were hot. His friend believed him worthy of trust, and he was somewhat worthy, though he eventually pawned both chess set and crystal vase.

At the bass's foot was a book borrowed from his daughter (*The Idiot's Guide to Personal Finance*) and another from the adjunct (Marlowe's *Doctor Faustus*, though he had meant to take a biography of John Milton). Around dusk, he sat in his recliner and stared into them. He watched the evening news and Wheel of Fortune. Pat and Vanna had retained their looks for decades because they were made of plastic. Berg would not have minded a little plastic in him, with his scalp itchy and afire, and police lights flashing through the blinds. The cops were almost always outside, always after someone else. He stared into the glass.

(Then he wanted a drink. Then he called me. Then he wanted to call his daughter. I said, Don't. He didn't. Then he wanted to go see the adjunct. I said, Don't. He did.)

He found the adjunct on her bed, slashing at student papers with her pen. She made room for him to join her, but she did not return his greeting, much less remark on his barren head.

White particle board shelves crowded the wall on the bed's guest side. They were tightly packed with books of English Renaissance poetry and criticism that had been lovingly boxed and unboxed in move upon move. She taught not literature but composition to stoners to whom scansion must have sounded like a video game's title. She broadcast their misspellings and misapprehensions on various social media sites. The shelves and bed (a queen) bordered a path of brownish carpet so narrow he had to either sidewind down it or crawl the bed's length to the pillow. He chose the latter method.

She kept a bottle of Shiraz and a mug on a low plastic nightstand. During her second or third serving, she would often hold the mug with both hands and wish aloud that she had kept her baby. She said it would have made her less bitter toward the world or motivated her to finish writing her book or eat a more balanced diet. It would have consoled her for the disappointing scents and brains of her students. Berg generally kept quiet during these outpourings.

That night, however, he said that years of parenthood had not diminished his fear of his daughter's faith in him. The girl asked for his advice no matter what he broke. He loved her, he said, though he couldn't prove it anymore. He thought a better father would have pushed her to love someone else.

The adjunct handed him the bottle, lifted the mug, and invited him to make a toast. He gritted his teeth and declined. (I had warned him a thousand times against woman drinkers.)

She recited: "For inward light alas/Puts forth no visual beam."

She kept cinnamon candles burning in the bathroom whether or not anyone's bowels had been voided within the hour. Their scent wafted under the door and intermixed with anything left exposed for more than a few minutes. It had infused the sheets and shelves and silverware with hints of breakfast. It filled her mouth.

He enjoyed more the way her breasts made his hands feel large.

When they finished, she resumed the War on Dumb. He said it was hard enough to sleep with lamps on, much less the noise of her shuffling papers and scribbling comments. She said that she alone had signed the lease, so she would do in here what she damn well pleased.

He asked if he looked new to her.

Hm, she said.

He pointed to his head.

She clicked buttons on her phone. He wondered if she was relaying to the world a student's idiocy or his own.

In the morning, Berg helped her remove the covers. Midway through the job, he blanked over not the mattress's giant blue snowflake pattern but the overlying yellow stain. It summed up something, but he couldn't say what. She snapped him back to the chore at hand.

(A week later he and I met for coffee. The barista moved me, though she wouldn't meet my eyes. Berg wasn't interested. His new hair looked like the fuzz on a baby chick, but it was gray and probably coarse, because he scratched it every few minutes. He said he hadn't wanted to drink too often since he had left the adjunct's apartment.

Good, I said.

He tapped his forehead against the table. He wept. I worried that the barista would eye me right then, and that she would think me responsible for this quivering goop, but she didn't, thank God.

That's normal, I said.)

His daughter and her roommate had overfilled their drawing room with their enthusiasms. Golden flowers drooped across tables and bookshelves. Wires ran from the large mounted TV to a laptop and an iPad port standing on two columns of textbooks pressed together. Their couch and recliner set, like the TV, had been gifts from the roommate's parents. One of his daughter's gossip magazines was splayed spine up on the chair's right arm. At the couch's left foot were three buckets of yarn. The roommate crocheted potholders in her spare time. Some were mosaics of color; others were emblazoned with Christian iconography. The pair of them had tacked to the back wall hundreds of prints and portraits of flowers, party times, and the roommate's savior.

The kitchen was speckled with breadcrumbs. Its refrigerator had a TV-ad look, crammed with meats and cheeses and fruits and cabbage heads. He bent toward the corks of two bottles of Riesling set side by side. He noted their resemblance to nipples. Meat juice had dried stickily to the fridge's bottom.

The roommate's finished potholders filled a counter drawer. From it, she had pulled her gift to him. She said maybe Jesus would lead him elsewhere. But the shaving had been her idea.

Their pantry was bursting with sacks of white, light brown, and dark brown sugar as well as cornstarch and flour and baking soda; tubs of raisins and prunes; tall, thin boxes of pasta; jars of tomato sauce; cans of assorted beans and fruits; bags of rice, almonds, walnuts, and potato chips; tins of sugar cookies; cases of soda; Tupperware containers of chocolate cereal and one of Raisin Bran, which she kept for his visits. She teased him about his hair while he poured himself a bowl. Her eyes were red.

They took seats at either end of the plush drawing room couch. Its pillows were oversized, overstuffed squares covered in daisy prints. She loved this monster couch, but he found its cushions too soft and swallowing. He couldn't eat while it ate him. He set his bowl on the end table. There he saw "tonite!" (*sic*, tonight) scripted on a sticky note. He wondered about her plans.

On the coffee table, nestled among their blondest flowers, were two framed photos: one of the roommate's family and the other of his daughter's mother. His daughter asked if she should ask about his new look.

He said he had made a mistake, as usual.

She nodded.

He said her eyes were red.

She said her roommate had recently prosed (*sic*, proposed) to her the act of love, and that she had accepted it, but she had not conserved (*sic*, considered) her boyfriend, and now she felt rough misery in this apartment, as though each item in it had gained a scouring pad's texture. Is that, she asked, what happened with him and Mama?

Berg couldn't answer. He was picturing the (lovely) roommate disrobed in his daughter's bedroom. Above her (innie) belly button, the roommate had a birthmark in the shape of Cuba. In this vision, candles burned love into being. His daughter sat on her fine brass bed (a king), with its imposing headboard and frilly canopy, its purple sheets with high thread counts. Beside the bureau, the (lovely enough) adjunct shredded "tonite!" She unzipped her dress and brought a canister of shaving cream to the bed. The roommate delivered a razor. His daughter relaxed among a bevy of pillows. Berg felt unconscionably tight down low. He excused himself.

In the bathroom, the hair of at least three people was conspicuous and curled along every surface. It floated on gray scum at the tub's base. He toweled it nearly dry. Short, dark hairs lay in a ring around the sink's drain. His daughter's boyfriend might have stayed over the previous night, or the roommate had another man of her own. Berg wiped out the sink and washed his hands.

He found orange congealments on the shower walls and supposed that he and his daughter were bonded by at least one benign thing.

A wire shelving unit hung from the showerhead. It held soaps, loofahs, pumice stones, and razors. He knew the longest and bluest razor belonged to her roommate. The man's razor was as cheap as his.

He stalled for a while in the shower. If he could have recalled his daughter's mother's bedroom, he might have gone out and laid bare the misused world to his daughter, but he had visited that bedroom and a hundred others under the influence of no small amount of wine. His memories of those days were a pile of torn clothes in a dark closet. He felt drunk blind trying to sort them: sex toys; diaries; textbooks; acoustic guitars; pencils; teddy bears; underwear molding on a window unit A/C; Xerox paper; batteries; floppy discs; drawers half-pulled and others fully pulled from chests; boxes of aspirin; bottles of antidepressants; an empty box of diapers; a dog moaning all through the human act of love; snippets of schoolgirl poetry read aloud by someone and to which he nodded along; the light of a neighboring Dairy Queen spilling through curtains; a partner's tooth coming loose on his tongue; the feel of a fifth hand under the sheets. How could he needle these dark scraps into a presentable hair shirt? That was the roommate's talent.

He pushed and pushed against the shower walls.

At the good-bye, he encouraged his daughter to think of an apartment as a test of character which he had too often failed. She gave him a clipped flower, its stem wrapped in foil, to put in a vase. He said he didn't own a vase. Take it, she said. At home, he set the flower in a glass of water and found a note crumpled inside the foil. She had written that, in general, the older the shaving man, the likelier it was that his hare (*sic*, hair) would return in humiliating patches, but, from what she could tell, his hare (twice!) was coming back all over. She must have read about it in one of her magazines. He poured himself a bowl of Raisin Bran. He didn't know where she was, but he thanked her again and again.

(I will not describe the roommate's bedroom. I will not say how long Berg's hair remained atop her bed, whether on a pillow or in its center, or when it was swept into a bin.

I confess that I have grown ashamed at how coldly I have shared Berg's confidences with you. I confess as well that the cheap razor in the shower belonged to me. Also, I slept with the adjunct last weekend. Then I stole her biography of Milton. That poet troubles me. His certainty of his personal genius and his Christ never faltered. I have called myself a genius only in moments of petty self-loathing, as when I have forgotten to buy soap at the grocery. I have felt the presence of God in no room at no time no matter how much I have yearned.

For instance, one night, years ago, my car quit east of New Orleans. Almost no one who answered my call wanted to help. My father heard me slurring through the phone and said I could swim the lake for all he cared. But my uncle drove to me from his home in Chalmette. When I hopped in his pick-up, he handed me two aspirins and a thermos of cool water. Gospel music played low in the driving background.

This uncle had designed and built his house, selected every board and wire, put screws rather than nails in the walls. A huge bay window gave him a wide view of his acreage, including the birdhouses he had hung from the limbs of a giant oak. Well-known and rare birds alike flew down for his expensive seed. Ten concrete posts held the house a full story above ground. The inspector had called it the safest structure on the Gulf Coast. A cot waited for me inside.

At breakfast, he served eggs, sausage, coffee, two more aspirins, and a bible. He had built the table, too, and had given the pine a rich, dark stain. He hunted deer in the woods out back. He skinned them and roasted the meat on fires he set in his yard. He had the untoned bigness of a warehouse foreman, the glorious hair and beard of an aging wizard. I am describing the only man I have ever known who could be of use at civilization's end. Yet if that end came as he believed it would, he would be raptured beforehand, so go figure. He would be one of innumerable points of light singing Hallelujah, while you and I would be prostrate before a dead TV.

I thought God had helped him build this house. I wanted one of my own. I didn't mind where he was about to lead this conversation.

He said we arrived empty to life. Everybody needed filling.

I know, I said.

He opened his book and went on.

I hungered for his Lord to enter my heart.

I starved at his table.

I quit drinking some months later. I still blame him for that.)

More Fish than Man

My cousin and I once fished under an interstate, where a bent leg of swamp lay exposed and easy to approach. Its water was nothing to drink, but it held plenty to eat. We caught a couple catfish inside half an hour. Then this gator came after his cork. My cousin has always been the mannest man I know, so of course he reeled in fast, hoping the gator would follow his line to our shore. When the gator turned away, he cast his line after it and nearly thumped it between the eyes. It gnashed its mean yellow teeth and beat the water into wicked green foam. My cousin kept reeling and casting till at last the gator did steal the cork.

"Some fun," my cousin said.

"You hear a dog?" I said.

That almost distracted him from the spoonhead of urine darkening my jeans. We went on fishing and pretending we were alike, but I had been revealed a mush to his solid, a shadow to his man.

A few months later, he went for a tour in Iraq. He returned scratch-free, and his wife called him a hero. So did I, and still do, in my pitiful heart.

Last Thanksgiving, I had to see him again. His fifth-grader son could shoot a pistol on target. That's how American they were.

I should not envy him. My wife jogs four miles every morning to maintain her wondrous body. Her spirit, too, is quite rare. After the neighbor's kitten had been poisoned, she conducted a service that wet the eyes of almost every man, woman, and child on our block. Three days ago, she drew my head to her bosom and read aloud poems by Milton and Donne in her angel's voice. And my daughter holds my finger in this singular way. She sings nonsense about fairies and birds. She gives me presents of leaves during walks through our neighborhood. Love grants us too many favors to disdain it absolutely, but it reduces every thought of the future to worry over who might run whom into a ditch.

The night before the holiday, for instance, I had to pin my daughter to the ground and pry open her mouth with one hand so I could brush her teeth with the other. My wife kept her back against the bed's headboard throughout the ordeal. She crocheted a beanie and turned up the volume on her headphones so she wouldn't feel herself an accomplice to torture.

A man could do many things after that, but what, in a hotel room? I tried the Christian bible once again but could not get past the opening of the opening gospel's record of lineage: ____ who begat ____ who begat _____ ad nearly infinitum. I understood those early church people had to prove their case, but they could have used a better hook.

After my family fell asleep, I went to buy an ice cream sandwich and found the desk clerk thumbing through a change purse messy with purple diamonds. He arranged its cards into three columns. I fast-walked to the nearby freezer and handled several ice cream sandwiches as though the quality of one could be compared and contrasted with that of others. I did not want to deal with any man engaged in crime, particularly one who filled out a company Polo shirt with that many muscles. Also, he wore a gold chain necklace and matching hoop earrings. To be fair, he had a soft, intelligent voice. That evening, he had given my daughter a beach ball to bounce through the lobby. He had charm. Yet I did not approach the counter until he had pocketed the cards he wanted and tucked away the change purse.

"You'll want an apple," he said. He touched a wicker basket that held about a dozen grannies.

"No, thanks. Got a sweet tooth tonight."

"Apple's got sugar too. It's so late, you probably shouldn't have sugar at all. But if you gonna have sugar, it ought to be natural. None of that fake stuff."

I bargained my way into purchasing both.

I ate the ice cream sandwich on my return to the room, and would have eaten the apple too, but I found a Chihuahua in a crate outside someone's door. The dog yipped and snapped at the cage. I whispered a curse at it. No one came out to get it or to apologize. Soon I was safe in our room, but I had never quietly eaten a snack, and my loves were snoring, so I tiptoed into the bathroom. I admired its thorough whiteness. Even the used linens, curled like pets asleep on the floor, added to its elegance.

Yet, rather than eat, I unscrewed the sink's gasket. I did not find in the drain the expected four-winged stopper. The gasket had instead been screwed into a piece of cork suitable for fishing or sexual kink. It squealed as I drew it up the drain. It was dirty with unstrung coils of hair and beads of sewage like caviar. Hard to believe we had not noticed the cork plugging the drain in pursuit of our evening toiletries, but I had not, in fact, brushed my teeth or washed my hands since the previous morning. I cannot speak for what my wife did or did not do with the bathroom door shut. The trouble with my daughter had occurred far from the sink, on the floor between our bed and her cot.

I could have made my cousin sound worse, during that gator story, by saying that a strong fisherman resists the temptation of a cork. Such a fisherman trusts himself to feel the prey's tug. He wants the competition to be, as much as possible, between himself and the fish, but there are few strong fishermen in the world. My new cork had an orange stripe, like that of a gym sock, around its wide end. The stripe offers a supplementary signal to the weakest fishermen, who must see both cork and color vanish before they can believe there is a fish wriggling on their line. Even then, one might confuse a fish's strike with a current's pull. I might be more fish than man.

That clerk could have accepted my money without grazing my downturned palm with an upturned index finger. He could have. He did, however, sell me the apple I needed.

After breakfast, my wife let me stay at the hotel to sleep off a purported headache. She would pick me up that afternoon, in time to gorge. Once she and my daughter had gone, I used a nail file to shave the cork and apple into slivers which I tore into shreds. These I mashed into a kind of paste. Again I came upon the dog in its crate outside that door. Again it barked all through my approach. Again no one came to help me. I squatted and pressed the paste through the thin metal grating. The dog nipped at my hand but could not wound me deeply enough. I returned to my room and waited another hour before calling my wife. On my way to meet her, I saw that the crate had been removed.

My cousin wore an American flag pin to dinner, but I withstood its shine and him too, perhaps because his son overturned the bowl of cranberry sauce and had to be taken outside, while my daughter served as a model of obedience. Perhaps, but, after dark, I found the clerk outside the hotel pool's entrance. I bummed a cigarette. A hard breeze lifted the tails of our jackets. It swept a plastic bag over the water. He took my hand. His index finger—each of his fingers, I soon learned—had a new and thrilling callus.

Known and Unknown Records of Kip Winger

Those who remember Kip Winger likely believe he is either dead or, at best, managing a fast food franchise in rural California. He spins and gyrates in their memories as the handsome lead singer and bassist of the hair metal band that bore his last name. Over the past thirty years, however, he has led a surprising variety of musical projects, few of which required him to show off his chest, perm his hair, squeeze into spandex, and make sex moves and eyes for a camera.

Bergen rarely thought of Kip until his father sent him five emails, rabbinic-sounding interpretations of the musician's life and discography. The following sample, from the first email, regarded Winger's eponymous debut (Atlantic Records, 1987): *We learn from these riffs and strums the truth of Winger. He came like an angel, knowing we would be jealous of him. So he sang and played. That he never played bass in a video does not mean he could not play. Believe he played. Believe he has always played. Believe he always will.*

Both Bergen and his wife Eva knew what the emails meant. His father had returned to town for hugs and forgiveness, Bergen had denied him both, and now the chance had been lost. Her husband's hard heart moved her to break several dishes against a wall.

She might have been looking for an excuse. Her patience had dripped away since the bauble had been lost. Two years prior, she had gone with her college girls to Mardi Gras and drank and probably flashed her way through New Orleans. She said she had caught the bauble at the Zulu parade. That story, to Bergen's mind, remained open to question. The bauble held such merit in her heart. She called it an emerald, though anyone could see its glass shell had been injected with green dye.

She also hated the sheaves of paper that for weeks had been growing atop their tables, under chairs and the sofa, behind toilets, in the mop bucket. The paper clogged drains and air vents throughout the house. It came in all sizes and shapes, up to and including centagons. Eva threatened a bonfire in the backyard, but Bergen was not overly troubled by the accumulation. Sometimes, he pulled the handle on his recliner, eased back, and imagined the way two sheets might make love and spawn in the air duct. They would scratch at each other till a baby sheet peeled away from its mother. That image transported him elsewhere.

Other times, he would read philosophy. One evening, he came upon a line that led him to wonder if Aristotle had predicted his father: "The musical is an accident of man." The Big Greek Mind had scribbled that idea two thousand years ago. A toilet musing, Bergen thought. He pictured the BGM on an ancient bucket, distinguishing between essential legs and inessential loves, finding a hint of Bergen's father in his morning stink. The BGM would then write a penetrating truth about the smell. Bergen set down his book and wrote "stale loaf" on a piece of blue construction paper. Daytime TV suggested that loafers like his father were widespread, that his bread had no special grain. He crumpled the paper and threw it atop the pile at his feet. He wondered if the BGM had foreseen hair metal. If the BGM had anticipated Winger, had he also realized that music might be less an accident of man and more one of his time? How much had he guessed of our time? How often had his wipes been tainted by despair?

Like any parent, Bergen had felt wet earth in his baby's diaper. He had been so careless at some wipings that he later found cold brown shavings in his arm hair. He had failed to pass them off as unwashed paint. Once, when Joel was newly born and soiling himself every third hour, Bergen poked and dabbed at the baby's waste, let its scentless death chill get under his nails. He learned too much thereby.

His father claimed, in the second email, to have drunk Coronas with Kip and guitarist Paul Taylor on Jacksonville Beach in 1985. The sun was already baking the sand that morning, so they gathered under a rainbow umbrella, where his father described a quandary in which a woman was curved and willing but was not a woman in the legal sense. The men decided that the question depended on more than curves. His father described the hair, face, and smile of a checkout girl from the grocery. Everyone agreed that, if she was willing, okay.

They drank. Waves came tenderly on the beach. The sun made the men wet and golden. At least one of them did not think a theft was imminent.

Six years later, Bergen's father left him for Oakland, California. Bergen liked to picture his father burning hours at an efficiency apartment's counter with an unsipped mug of coffee before him, mouthing the lyrics to "Seventeen."

That evening, after Bergen rejected "stale loaf," Eva sat on the sofa and stretched her legs before him. He admired them and her exposed, glittered chest. The butterfly tattoo on her left breast had a tongue of glitter. She asked him why he bothered about the old man or Winger anymore. That was over. Why not bother her? Her legs extended silky and modelesque from a purple skirt that was too short and out of place in a family home. He imagined them grooving on a pole in a smoky room or emerging from a limousine. Her feet were bare. Her toes had been polished a deep and inviting shade of red. And, of course, she was topless and glittered. He said he was very bothered.

"Bother me," she said.

But Joel stomped in with his red truck, cleared paper until there was an oval of play space available, and wheeled the truck in crescents over the rug. Beyond his wheeling left arm, the boy sat like a Buddha. He wore footie pajamas with a monkey on the butt, made of gentle material Bergen could not name.

Eva folded her arms over her chest. "You're no fun," she said.

He shrugged. "What do you want me to do?"

"Be fun."

"We're not in college anymore."

"I know."

She wasn't happy to know it. She sent someone, maybe her lush sister, a text message.

Soon she put on a t-shirt, carried Joel upstairs to the nursery, and attempted a lullaby. The boy rarely slept to her song. Sometimes he slept in his crib, but more often with either parent beside him on the carpet. Bergen and his wife once spent a night together with the child coughing on the floor between them. More than once, Bergen walked four-plus miles worth of house with the child slung over his shoulder. He and Eva never considered taking the child into their bed.

After fifteen minutes, Bergen relieved his wife of the shrieking boy. He touched her arm. She did not wish him luck. Bergen spread over the carpet a blanket emblazoned with Dale Earnhardt, Sr.'s racing number three, a gift from the lush sister. Then he approached the crib. "Calm," Bergen whispered. "Calm, calm, calm." He carried Joel into the hall and whispered and felt his power work on the boy. Eva had no such power. It scared Bergen as much as it hurt her, because he was not sure how much he loved this child. He thought Joel's face might one day freeze in a pout. Even when pleased with dinner, the kid had a grimace to him. Strangers called him cute, but Bergen found it hard to muster great hope for the boy's dating and career prospects.

Two rooms down, Eva was probably drawing back the bedsheets. Bergen resented how easily she could sleep without him. In her dreams, she was often both herself and either Norma Talmadge or Lillian Gish, and almost always she wandered in a maze of steel bushes, hearing a woman sing and being unable to sing a reply. Her dreams bored him. He suspected they bored her too, but they had little else to discuss at breakfast. Perhaps he should have interrupted her that morning with news of his eggs. He had smelled his future in them. It was a familiar smell, though no less fearful for it. More, because he knew he would be left with the boy.

The third email developed a flattering contrast between the guitar solos of Reb Beach and Eddie Van Halen. The more alluring fourth was composed of short biographies of Winger video models. It included the successful transition of the Mediterranean beauty who had closed the "Can't Get Enough" video from professional model to assistant manager of a Bank of America on Jacksonville's south side. From that branch, Bergen had recently acquired a loan application and handshake promise of the lowest interest rates in town, as well as a profile shot of her which, as a result of his having to aim and fire his phone's camera without alarming her, her co-workers, the security guard, and the customer with the pedophilic grin, included the shadow of his left forefinger on her neck. Her body was hidden behind the counter, but one could nonetheless make out the high cheekbones and igniter eyes that had once made her a fine subject for adolescent thought.

Bergen carried Joel down the mercifully unpapered stairs. He tiptoed over the construction paper and brown grocery bags mounded everywhere on the first floor, taking his son through the living room, dining room, and kitchen, then down the hall, past the half-bathroom, utility closet, and laundry room. Upstairs, he had to plant his feet with every step to keep from slipping on unspooled toilet paper. He took his son past the closed door of the master bedroom, and then the office, from which graph paper spilled under the door, before returning to the nursery. He whispered, "Calm, calm, calm" throughout their journey. The power did not rest in the word but in his patient repetition of it. He set his son on top of the blanket and snuggled him there.

The fifth email sketched Kip's own biography, including the surprising fact that Kip had spent several years as a widower. Bergen worried about neither this wife Beatrice's death nor Kip's unbottomed grief. He wondered instead how any shift of circumstances might have altered minor musical history. Suppose, for example, that Beatrice had not died in a car crash in 1996. Would Kip have nonetheless reformed his band that year to play a more progressive brand of chicken soup rock? Suppose he had married Beatrice in 1985 rather than 1991. Would he have still been so interested in Bergen's father's description of a checkout girl? Would he have turned out the second-rate schlock for which he remains most famous? Would he agree with Bergen's judgment that it was second rate even for hair metal? Suppose Beatrice had grown pregnant before the band completed its debut album. Would Kip have been so ready to market the pilfered "Seventeen," particularly if he knew his child was going to be a daughter, or would he have cashed in anyhow? Would he have been wise enough to invest the money earned from that single in a college fund for the girl, or were college funds not yet an option for parents, or would his hairspray have toxically short-circuited any mature decision-making on his part? Would Kip have left a living Beatrice for his second wife Paula? Would he have heard the loving uuuggghhh of stationery in the wall behind the watercolor painting of boats above Joel's crib? Did Kip offer a bauble to either his first or second or Bergen's own wife as a closing seduction move? Suppose both Beatrice and the imaginary unborn child died in a car crash in early 1987. Would the tragedy have compelled him to drop hair metal for classical music, or would he have gone ahead with the album, perhaps only improving the lyrics to "Headed for a Heartbreak"? Would that question be too cheap to pose to Kip, a revelation of Bergen's low wit at a late hour, when he found himself wide awake and dumb?

Joel turned and faced him. The boy was Bergen in miniature and, too, the darkest mass in the dark room. Bergen was expected, come daylight, to resume filling the boy with facts, to show him that this was a truck and it was red and it had wheels and the wheels could be counted and so forth. He was compelled to dispense fact upon fact, day after day, year upon year, until the boy had enough of them to graduate with a practical degree; hold a meaningful job with a high salary and generous benefits; win the esteem of his peers; love without reservation a well-suited partner of his choosing; and treat him, Bergen, with respect. Bergen wasn't sure either he or the boy wanted to do any of that.

And he did not know how much he could teach beyond the basic characteristics of a toy truck. He suspected more than understood the world. He doubted, for instance, the existence of any one BGM, imagining rather a composite build-up of toilet musings written by a host of dead Greeks, maybe as part of a long con or joke extending from Attica to the heavenly sphere. Bergen might tell his son that, in the afterlife, Greeks hang out in a dim buffet room and wait for the philosophically inclined, newly dead to turn up the light so they can laugh and laugh. Then they offer their victims fried fish and green beans. Bergen would have to explain how an afterlife might work and how green beans could get to heaven while starches could not and how a dead man could eat fried fish even though his beaten body had been left for real fish to eat under lapping waves.

Joel moaned, pulled Bergen's lip, and screamed.

"Calm," Bergen said. "Calm, calm." He stood and carried the boy to the upstairs bathroom and turned on the faucet and said, "Calm." The water sound helped on some hard nights but, that night, he found the tub full of origami paper folded into cranes, so the water sounded like rain falling on rocks and through the gaps between them. Joel cried until the paper went soft and pasty in the dark. Then they heard the old strike of water on tub and calmed enough to return to the number three blanket.

The year his father drank with half the band, Bergen's mother left and he, Bergen, wore Skywalker Underoos. Soon Laura's smoke breath settled into their furniture. The rest of her dominated the TV and ice cream. She and his father played air guitar to music videos till she rambled on for good. Bergen's father rambled west shortly thereafter. But, when things were still hot between them, Bergen would come in from school, and his father would say, "Hang with us." Bergen always declined. Laura's love sounds ran nightly through the walls. She wore purple pants tight and diaphanous as Saran-Wrap. Bergen stole them from the wash and kept them under his mattress.

In 2000, Kip released *Songs from the Ocean Floor* (Meadowlark Music), a solo album dedicated to his lost Beatrice. It had lighter sounds, counterpoints, even clarinets. He sang that he had "crossed a sea of crippling pain," but loss had not sucked him down black holes or overmuch into Jesus. He became, instead, a more sincere-sounding heartthrob.

Last week, Bergen's father signed a lease for an efficiency apartment somewhere—maybe he had returned to Oakland or migrated to Israel—and affected a Rabbi's beard and learning. *I study Winger more deeply and extensively than anyone else. I try to stay humble among its tunes, for Winger is endless, for Winger is Wisdom. Its Wisdom is the fragrance of a lemon. The lemon loses nothing at your sniffing. Or is lemonade drawn from other citrus somehow?* Bergen imagined his father rocking out on the Dead Sea's beach, headphones on, a private ecstasy whirling in him, strangers floating on dense saltwater, a poodle advancing on him from the left.

The entire month before, his father had slept on a trundle bed in the family's office, and three of the home's four occupants enjoyed their time together. Joel giggled at his grandfather's beeping nose game. Eva appreciated the new source of rock knowledge, and the two of them shared concert stories. During those weeks, Bergen had been little more than a presence at the table or, once, at a neighborhood dive so low that a cat slept on the bar top and its fleas jumped from it to Bergen's hand and back again. There his father said, to the bottles lined behind the bar, that Eva was more lover than mom. Her legs were built for leaving.

Bergen slapped at the fleas. He, too, addressed the liquor. He said that it was difficult to enjoy Merlot in a hole like this.

His father said, "You're not supposed to drink Merlot in here. I told you that from the start."

They finished their drinks, but not before Bergen suffered a black waking dream in which a shirtless Kip photographed Eva's breasts, handed her the bauble, and hummed a line which moved her from the bar to his convertible.

Now Bergen imagined her crumpling paper on their bedroom floor, hurt over the bauble and tired of his brain, as was he. Then reading a text message summarizing her lush sister's dating advice. Then on the bed and touching herself with Kip in mind. Then pressing buttons on her phone to transfer a sum of money from their joint savings account into a personal one whose existence Bergen guessed only that moment. Bergen wanted his son to be awake and wheeling that red truck and in that right mindfulness. He wanted to ask his son, "Will you love me enough to drain a colostomy bag?"

Kip stunned anyone paying attention with his symphony *Ghosts* (2010). It was performed as a ballet in San Francisco and elsewhere. Bergen's father might have seen the show or waited behind the theatre, hoping to stab the thief in each blue eye. Bergen had streamed this record several times in leaden moods with a mostly unmoved chest. Yet its adagio sometimes recurred to him when he showered. He even hummed a lathering bar or two. The music almost wiped his brain clean.

Bergen imagined that, one morning, after honey cakes and wine, the BGM went to his bucket. Too close by, he found a doomed mutt with worms moving in its torn leg. It prematurely stank the ground. The BGM knew that leaving begat leaving. He lifted his toga, sat, and heard Kip's adagio in the poor dog's wound. Sonic mountains and seas! Arranged to the last foreign note! Bright future! Lemon thoughts helped him through the next ten minutes.

Joel made a kind of whistle, then swelled, then stiffened. In such moments, when Bergen knew his son wouldn't dream much longer no matter how much Bergen whispered, "Calm," because in the boy's diaper grew a brown pancake that no one could abide—in such moments, Bergen wanted to know anything else.

He left his son in order to dig around the office for the bauble. His desk and bookshelves had gone under a chaos of paper: long ribbons of parchment; crumpled balls of onionskin; rectangles of both standard and corrugated cardboard; assorted grades of sandpaper, some of which had been used and left him lightly sawdusted; mulberry paper with a sickly sweet, almost-pine scent; poster board cut into stars and phase-shapes of the moon; sheets of cardstock heavy as dictionaries; and innumerable confetti, every dot of which bore his father's first initial. When Laura left, the old man made a bed of the carpet and watched *Dial MTV* and mouthed insults at bands he loathed. When Winger came on, his mouth grew wet. His eyes flickered. Bergen interrupted him one afternoon. His father patted the ground. "Hang with me," he said. Bergen did. They baked frozen pizzas and washed them down with soda and played air guitar long into the night. Two days later, his father wrote him a short letter and left for Oakland.

In the second month of his wife's pregnancy, Bergen came home early from work with a bouquet of yellow carnations. Eva napped on the couch with an open mouth and, around her neck, a gold chain with the bauble attached. Her hands rested beneath a bedsheet. His chest moved. A movie him might have strewn the petals over her dreaming body or burned them in the backyard and let their foodie neighbors smell his cooking heart. But he clipped the flowers and set them in a vase and drove alone through their neighborhood, tapping the steering wheel to the beat of radio songs. He had seen a similar bauble around the neck of the ex-starlet branch manager, though his finger had smudged the evidence.

The office had so thickened with scrap that he could not reach the carpet to feel around. He got paper cuts up and down his arms. Twice, he confused the edge of a book for the bauble. Meanwhile, his father stood on the Dead Sea's beach and enjoyed the way the morning sun broke on the water. Meanwhile, Kip, alone in his private studio, played bass, the same notes he had played for Beatrice, the same notes he had hummed in Eva's ear.

Perhaps Eva too, down the hall, under the sheets, once again heard those notes. Perhaps she was sprinkling herself with fresh glitter or putting on diaphanous pants and a top that showed a wing of the butterfly tattoo but hid the tongue of glitter. Perhaps she was steeling herself to climb out the window.

Bergen would have liked to stop her before she got too far down the oak tree. He would have liked to present the bauble and win back her love. He would have liked to bother her again and again. Failing that, he would have liked there to be a last straw, but last straws, he knew, were for more dramatic men. He had maintained steady employment with one firm for ten years and, no matter how hard his day had been at the office, had never gotten ripped after work and slapped his wife around. He never, in fact, drank more than his doctor recommended. His wife's lush sister drank too much on a particular Thanksgiving, pulled him into her parents' bathroom, tugged the waistband of her thong above her jeans, and asked if he appreciated its redness. He declined to answer. Bergen wished he could at least hurt his wife before she left. Bergen wished he had committed a series of escalating offenses, culminating that night in a last straw she would eventually share with some Fallen Pretty Boy because, in Bergen's wish, she would never again hook up with Kip. She and this FPB would be wobbly on neighboring barstools in a dive in a state like Arkansas. She would describe the straw with a hundred tears rather than a shrug.

She did leave, not that night but another, the night on which Joel at last slept well in his crib and the home was clean of paper and Bergen learned of the help that Alan Parsons and Alice Cooper had given to Kip's career in the mid-eighties. Or maybe she left the night Bergen listened to the Winger reunion albums back to back to back. He had his headphones turned up, he was tapping his foot, and he silently confessed that he enjoyed this music while Eva dragged a suitcase down the stairs. Or maybe she left on a bright afternoon two years from now, and he discovered the house empty of her and glitter when he brought Joel home from daycare. He ordered a pizza and, while waiting for it to arrive, he answered his son's barrage of questions with a barrage of words. Dinner itself was a quiet, gorging respite. Joel did not, however, want to watch cartoons afterward. He said, "Mama, Mama, Mama." Bergen whispered, "Calm, Calm, Calm," and carried him up and down the stairs and through the house until the child slept. Then Bergen hunted for a letter that did not exist.

He saw those and other futures while rummaging through the office. He understood that Eva would leave no matter how many baubles he found, but that understanding did not stop him in his search. Nor did he quit when he heard Joel cry out, when he knew his son needed him to change the loaded diaper and whisper, "Calm," when he knew that only his son could calm him. Paper moaned in the walls. A sheet of it snaked from the air vent. It was signed, "Dad." Then he remembered his father's short, useless letter: *I have done what I have done. All the rest is commentary.*

Acknowledgements

For Julie, Sam, and Miriam. You have given me everything.

For their hard work and general coolness: Duncan Barlow and everyone at Astrophil Press.

For everyone who read all or part of this book when it was just a dream of a manuscript: Sohrab Homi Fracis, Nicholas Grider, Christian TeBordo, Jennie Ziegler, Will Pewitt, Katy Mongeau, Alex Siwiecki, Annie DeWitt, and all the excellent readers at the Roxbury Writers Residency.

For the thinkers, sages, musicians, and writers whose work I have appropriated and manipulated in this book: Aristotle, Kip Winger, Rabbi Akiva, Rabbi Hillel, Samuel, John Milton, Donald Barthelme, and Blake Butler.

Credits

The stories in this collection were previously published in the following publications: "A Giving Toilet" in *Yalobusha Review*; "Good Fat" in *South Dakota Review*. "Archaeology of Dad" in *Prick of the Spindle*; "Harvest" (as "We Will Be Berries") in *Green Mountains Review*; "Cake" in *Heavy Feather Review*; "A Taste for Eel" in *Literary Orphans*; "Put that Thang in It Face" (as "Mannish") in *Crack the Spine*; "My Assets" in *The West Wind Review*; "Do the Fish" in *The Collagist*; "A Good Dog Would Forget" in *TheEEEL*; "The Blattarian Model" in *Menacing Hedge*; "Remainder" (as "A Closet in which Much Pride Has Been Taken") in *Interim*; "More Fish than Man" in *Heavy Feather Review*; and"Known and Unknown Records of Kip Winger" in *Juked*.

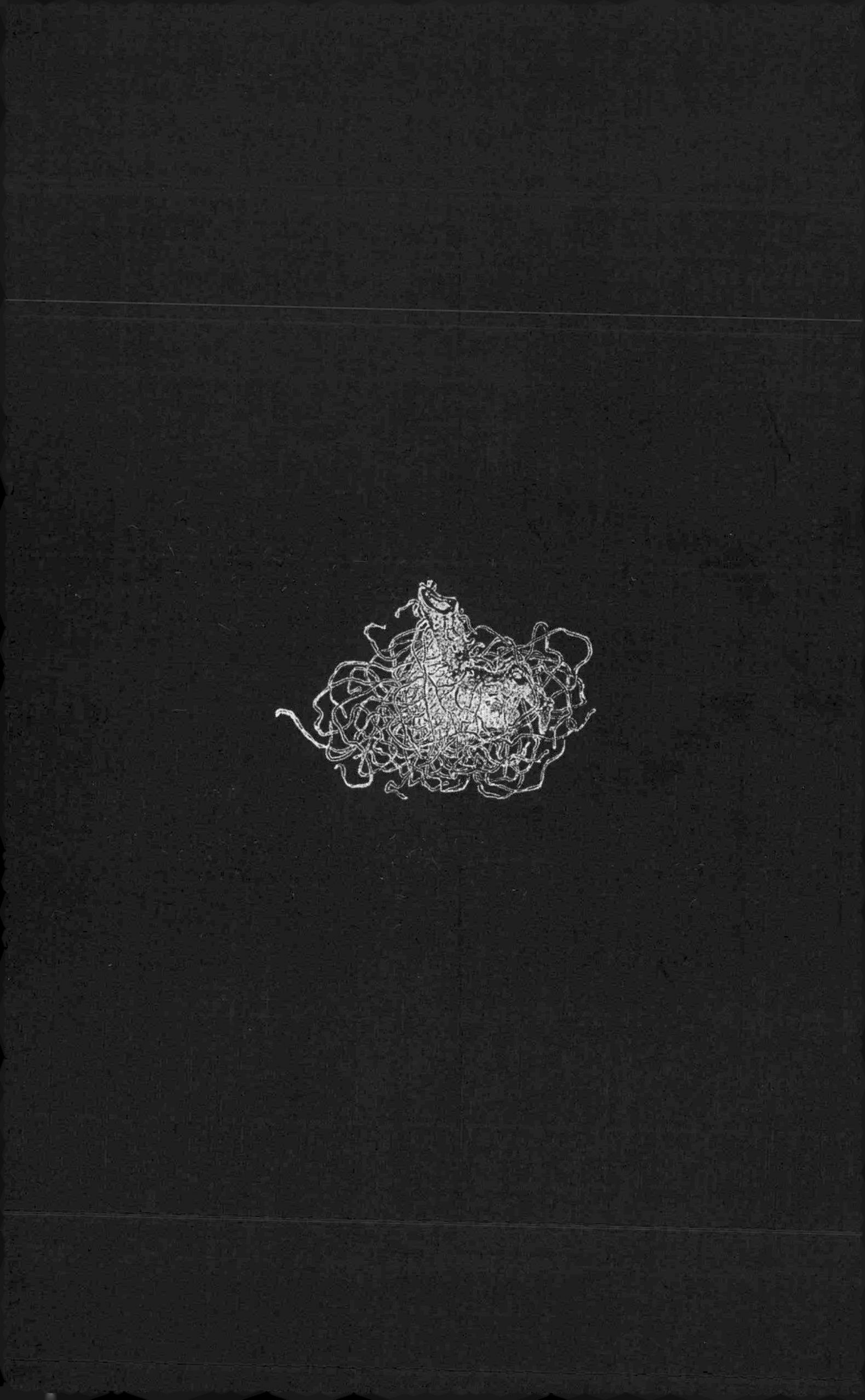